INTRODUCING ISSUES WITH OPPOSING VIEWPOINTS®

# Transportation Infrastructure

Lisa Idzikowski, Book Editor

I0869268

GREENHAVEN PUBLISHING

Published in 2021 by Greenhaven Publishing, LLC
353 3rd Avenue, Suite 255, New York, NY 10010

Copyright © 2021 by Greenhaven Publishing, LLC

First Edition

All rights reserved. No part of this book may be reproduced in any form without permission in writing from the publisher, except by a reviewer.

Articles in Greenhaven Publishing anthologies are often edited for length to meet page requirements. In addition, original titles of these works are changed to clearly present the main thesis and to explicitly indicate the author's opinion. Every effort is made to ensure that Greenhaven Publishing accurately reflects the original intent of the authors. Every effort has been made to trace the owners of the copyrighted material.

**Library of Congress Cataloging-in-Publication Data**

Names: Idzikowski, Lisa, editor.
Title: Transportation infrastructure / Lisa Idzikowski, book editor.
Other titles: Introducing issues with opposing viewpoints.
Description: First edition. | New York : Greenhaven Publishing, 2021. | Series: Introducing issues with opposing viewpoints | Includes bibliographical references and index. | Audience: Grades 7–12.
Identifiers: LCCN 2019058859 | ISBN 9781534507234 (library binding) | ISBN 9781534507227 (paperback)
Subjects: LCSH: Transportation—United States—Juvenile literature. | Infrastructure (Economics)—United States—Juvenile literature. | Transportation—Social aspects—United States—Juvenile literature.
Classification: LCC HE203 .T7545 2021 | DDC 388.0973—dc23
LC record available at https://lccn.loc.gov/2019058859

*Manufactured in the United States of America*

Website: http://greenhavenpublishing.com

# Contents

## Chapter 3: How Should Transportation Infrastructure Be Changed?

# Foreword

Indulging in a wide spectrum of ideas, beliefs, and perspectives is a critical cornerstone of democracy. After all, it is often debates over differences of opinion, such as whether to legalize abortion, how to treat prisoners, or when to enact the death penalty, that shape our society and drive it forward. Such diversity of thought is frequently regarded as the hallmark of a healthy and civilized culture. As the Reverend Clifford Schutjer of the First Congregational Church in Mansfield, Ohio, declared in a 2001 sermon, "Surrounding oneself with only like-minded people, restricting what we listen to or read only to what we find agreeable is irresponsible. Refusing to entertain doubts once we make up our minds is a subtle but deadly form of arrogance." With this advice in mind, Introducing Issues with Opposing Viewpoints books aim to open readers' minds to the critically divergent views that comprise our world's most important debates.

Introducing Issues with Opposing Viewpoints simplifies for students the enormous and often overwhelming mass of material now available via print and electronic media. Collected in every volume is an array of opinions that captures the essence of a particular controversy or topic. Introducing Issues with Opposing Viewpoints books embody the spirit of nineteenth-century journalist Charles A. Dana's axiom: "Fight for your opinions, but do not believe that they contain the whole truth, or the only truth." Absorbing such contrasting opinions teaches students to analyze the strength of an argument and compare it to its opposition. From this process readers can inform and strengthen their own opinions, or be exposed to new information that will change their minds. Introducing Issues with Opposing Viewpoints is a mosaic of different voices. The authors are statesmen, pundits, academics, journalists, corporations, and ordinary people who have felt compelled to share their experiences and ideas in a public forum. Their words have been collected from newspapers, journals, books, speeches, interviews, and the Internet, the fastest growing body of opinionated material in the world.

Introducing Issues with Opposing Viewpoints shares many of the well-known features of its critically acclaimed parent series, Opposing

Viewpoints. The articles allow readers to absorb and compare divergent perspectives. Active reading questions preface each viewpoint, requiring the student to approach the material thoughtfully and carefully. Photographs, charts, and graphs supplement each article. A thorough introduction provides readers with crucial background on an issue. An annotated bibliography points the reader toward articles, books, and websites that contain additional information on the topic. An appendix of organizations to contact contains a wide variety of charities, nonprofit organizations, political groups, and private enterprises that each hold a position on the issue at hand. Finally, a comprehensive index allows readers to locate content quickly and efficiently.

Introducing Issues with Opposing Viewpoints is also significantly different from Opposing Viewpoints. As the series title implies, its presentation will help introduce students to the concept of opposing viewpoints and learn to use this material to aid in critical writing and debate. The series' four-color, accessible format makes the books attractive and inviting to readers of all levels. In addition, each viewpoint has been carefully edited to maximize a reader's understanding of the content. Short but thorough viewpoints capture the essence of an argument. A substantial, thought-provoking essay question placed at the end of each viewpoint asks the student to further investigate the issues raised in the viewpoint, compare and contrast two authors' arguments, or consider how one might go about forming an opinion on the topic at hand. Each viewpoint contains sidebars that include at-a-glance information and handy statistics. A Facts About section located in the back of the book further supplies students with relevant facts and figures.

Following in the tradition of the Opposing Viewpoints series, Greenhaven Publishing continues to provide readers with invaluable exposure to the controversial issues that shape our world. As John Stuart Mill once wrote: "The only way in which a human being can make some approach to knowing the whole of a subject is by hearing what can be said about it by persons of every variety of opinion and studying all modes in which it can be looked at by every character of mind. No wise man ever acquired his wisdom in any mode but this." It is to this principle that Introducing Issues with Opposing Viewpoints books are dedicated.

# Introduction

*"Our nation is at a crossroads. Deteriorating US infrastructure is impeding our ability to compete in the thriving global economy, and improvements are necessary to ensure our country is built for the future. While we have made some progress, reversing the trajectory after decades of underinvestment in our infrastructure requires transformative action from Congress, states, infrastructure owners, and the American people."*

*—American Society of Civil Engineers,*
*Infrastructure Report Card, 2017*

What comes to mind when many people think about or hear the term transportation infrastructure? Do they think about great bridges like the Golden Gate in San Francisco, the Brooklyn Bridge in New York, or the Sunshine Skyway in Tampa? Do they think about airports like O'Hare in Chicago, JFK in New York, or Denver International in Denver? Or what about large, congested interstate highways such as I-405 in California, I-90 in Illinois, I-45 in Texas, or I-95 that runs almost 2,000 miles from the Canadian border south to Miami, Florida?

All of these examples meet the definition of transportation infrastructure, equipment and structures that a society needs in order to function. In the United States, many of these structures have been described as deteriorating, crumbling, in a state of disrepair, "like a third-world country," or falling apart. Many prominent people and organizations in the United States have declared that America's transportation infrastructure is, without question, in a horrible state of disrepair.

As the introductory quote states, the United States is on the brink of not being able to compete in a global economy because of the poor state of its infrastructure. The American Society of Civil Engineers (ASCE) is not the only outspoken source in this matter. In his February 2018 message to Congress, President Donald Trump said:

*Our Nation's infrastructure is in an unacceptable state of disrepair, which damages our country's competitiveness and our citizens' quality of life. For too long, lawmakers have invested in infrastructure inefficiently, ignored critical needs, and allowed it to deteriorate. As a result, the United States has fallen further and further behind other countries. It is time to give Americans the working, modern infrastructure they deserve.*

And Ray H. LaHood, who served as Secretary of the US Department of Transportation under President Barack Obama, has said that "America's infrastructure is like a third-world country," and that "We need big, big, resources. We need money. We need a big pot of money to get back to being number one in infrastructure."

How has this come about? Why has America's transportation infrastructure suffered over the decades? Can anything be done? None of these questions has an easy answer, but the American Society of Civil Engineers is one organization that thinks it is vitally important to address the issue. Since 1998, the twenty-eight civil engineers making up the committee that grades US infrastructure agree that America's infrastructure "is aging, underperforming, and in need of sustained care and action."

Anyone who has been stuck in a grid-locked traffic jam, a never-ending wait at an airport security check, or a busy train station, or who has heard of or experienced one of the bridge collapses or the water scandal in Flint, Michigan, would agree.

Transportation infrastructure is a vital component to communities, and it impacts everyone in society. Most people regularly drive private vehicles or use forms of public transportation that travel on interstate highways. Others hop on planes for business or pleasure. Some take trains, buses or boats to school or to work or to faraway destinations. Global trade and economic abilities in developed and developing countries depend on infrastructure that functions smoothly. And the health and safety of citizens can flourish or fail depending upon the condition of water systems, highways and bridges, airports, or hazardous and solid waste systems.

No one wants to suffer from inadequate or unsafe infrastructure. No one wants to be one of the approximately 40,000 people killed in yearly traffic accidents in the United States. Or to suffer from lead-tainted drinking water. Or to have been one of the almost 160 killed or injured in the 2007 bridge collapse in Minnesota. Obviously, people would rather enjoy the positive aspects of well planned and executed improvements in infrastructure. Better jobs and better pay because of public transportation that makes it convenient to reach places of employment. Better health because of dedicated bike lanes or walking paths for those that wish to not use cars. And better health when pollution is decreased because a lesser number of public transportation vehicles replaces the staggering number of private automobiles now is everyday use.

Something can and must be done to fix and improve the problems of transportation infrastructure now and into the future. A first step might be educating oneself about this controversial topic and realizing how importantly it affects us all. The current debate that surrounds this interesting topic is explored in the diverse viewpoints collected within *Introducing Issues with Opposing Viewpoints: Transportation Infrastructure*.

# Chapter 1

# Why Is Transportation Infrastructure Vital to Society?

*This image shows the variety of methods of transportation seen from one city block.*

Viewpoint 1

# Transportation Impacts Development and Shapes Economies

*"The reality is that transportation plays a broad role in shaping economies."*

## Paula Dowell

In the following viewpoint Paula Dowell argues that transportation plays a key role in shaping economies and development. The author analyzes specific areas in an economy that benefit from investment and improvement of transportation. Dowell also points out the ways that improved transportation helps both businesses and the public. Paula Dowell is an expert in the field of transportation economics.

### AS YOU READ, CONSIDER THE FOLLOWING QUESTIONS:

1. What are four ways that transportation affects economies, as stated by the author?
2. According to the author, how does transportation become beneficial for businesses?
3. Which public forms of transportation are important as seen in this viewpoint?

"The Top Five Ways Transportation Impacts Economic Development," by Paula Dowell, Ph.D., April 5, 2017. Reprinted by permission.

Traditionally, measuring return on investment for transportation initiatives has focused on direct user benefits and the economic impacts that arise from those cost savings. Estimating minutes of travel time saved by passengers or freight is acceptable, but some projects require more exploration and depth.

The reality is that transportation plays a broad role in shaping economies. Transportation:

- supports clusters and agglomerations;
- increases productivity;
- enhances jobs and labor market accessibility;
- opens new markets for businesses; and
- enhances supply chain efficiency.

Though not all transportation projects generate such benefits, some investments are considered strategic drivers of development. The economic impact of transportation projects can be measured in the benefits they bring to economic growth, job creation, trade facilitation, and the economies of scale created. Recognizing this reality is crucial because today's transportation needs far exceed available funding. Accordingly, transportation agencies at all levels of government seek to maximize their investments.

This is true despite the fact that, in 2015, the Fixing America's Surface Transportation (FAST) Act was signed into law. Included in the $305 billion authorized by the FAST Act is funding for critical public transportation, highway, and freight projects. There is an increased level of accountability in how transportation dollars are spent, so even with this money available, state, metropolitan, regional, and local agencies must justify the need, economic impact, and return on investment of their transportation investments. As such, it is important to assess transportation projects for their wider impact and use a sound economic analysis to make informed transportation decisions.

## Wider Impacts

Transportation investment impacts economic development in the following five ways:

*US roadways must be in excellent condition for goods to be transported around the country.*

## Supports Clusters and Agglomerations

Investment in transportation, especially transit, supports clusters and agglomerations in several ways. First, in large metropolitan areas, growth can be slowed when it is based only on automobile trips due to the limited downtown space. Effectively planned transportation can overcome this constraint and reinforce agglomerations by allowing more people to come closer together in higher density developments.

Second, the right transportation investments sustain clusters of industries and businesses by supporting their closer proximity to each other, improving productivity and creating clusters of activities. Finally, efficient transportation reduces the time distance between the suburbs, where some of the labor force lives, to the downtown areas.

## Increases Productivity

When transportation improvements increase the accessibility of people and businesses to reach jobs, services, goods, and activities, productivity also increases. This uptick may be due to reduced travel time and infrastructure enhancements. Because the labor market temporally is brought closer to their places of work due to improved travel time, businesses experience gains in worker productivity.

Business productivity is seen in other areas as well. For example, transportation improvements may improve freight delivery times. If truck drivers can reach their destinations more quickly, they can make more runs in their daily shifts, increasing their efficiency. Increasing worker and business productivity can in turn increase the productivity of the metropolitan area affected by the enhanced transportation system.

### Enhances Job and Labor Force Accessibility

Another economic benefit of transportation improvements is the resulting larger pool of employees available for the job market. This may come from a new transit or commuter rail line that makes it possible for employees to reach previously inaccessible jobs. Or, road improvements may decrease employees' travel time by car or bus. Overall, employers can better match employees with appropriate jobs based on the job requirements and employees' skills.

At the same time, new or improved transportation options increase the population's direct access to more job options, making an area more attractive. Given the importance that Millennials place on mobility and desire to forego car ownership, access to employment and recreation in walkable, bikeable, and transit-accessible areas is becoming a key factor for recruiting this critical workforce group.

## Opens New Markets for Businesses

New and improved transportation options do more than decrease the travel time or distance for commuters; they can be a factor in shifting the business sectors attracted to the metropolitan area. Building a multi-modal facility opens new markets for companies searching for locations with the appropriate transportation infrastructure for their corporate needs and manufacturing plants.

New rail, subway, and Metro lines attract new development—residential and commercial—providing businesses and passengers with more options to earn and spend their money. By improving access, enhanced transportation projects positively affect the economic impact of metropolitan areas.

## Enhances Supply Chain Efficiency

When businesses are clustered together, it is easier and quicker for them to reach their suppliers and customers. This phenomenon has a positive impact on freight logistics and delivery scheduling. Easier access to needed supplies and materials and faster delivery times to customers can help lower transportation and inventory carrying costs while increasing both productivity and profitability.

At the same time, improvements in the transportation infrastructure allow companies to expand their market reach and access to a larger customer base, which can increase their competitiveness.

By improving access to markets, goods and services, employment, housing, health care, and education while reducing the cost of moving people and goods, transportation projects can increase economic productivity and development.

## Assessing Economic Impact

While the benefits of travel time savings are substantial, the traditional method of measuring seconds saved per trip is outdated and insufficient. The investment in transportation contributes much more to the economy than the travel time savings alone. It is critical to quantify all of the productivity gains realized with enhanced transit, particularly in the current environment that seeks to maximize investment under the scrutiny of increased accountability. This is accomplished by assessing specific variables showing how the link among the economy, businesses, and commuters depends on the transportation system and how improvements affect productivity, income, and revenue.

Ideally, before and after studies would be conducted to measure the impact of new or improved transportation. However, these studies present inherent challenges due to the time lapse from project feasibility to the project opening. In addition, it is difficult to isolate the impact of the transportation infrastructure.

A better approach begins by ensuring that the stakeholders lead the project evaluation. This process involves conducting interviews with the transportation users, economic developers, and real estate personnel to learn and understand their perspectives and feedback on

## Fast Fact

**The American Society of Civil Engineers recommended in its latest report that the United States increase spending by $2 trillion in the next ten years on infrastructure and the economy.**

how an investment might change their behavior and impact development decisions. The information is used to determine travel demand and develop user costs and economic impact models.

The research yields the development of tools designed specifically to help understand the extent of the transportation project's impact on site selection, business attraction, and retention and economic development. The combination of expert knowledge, stakeholder input, and research also leads to better benefit-cost, economic impact, and return-on-investment analyses. This method of assessing transportation's economic impact leads to a more transparent, defensible, and intuitive analysis of the project.

## Return on Investment

Transportation, as one of the key costs of producing goods and services, is a major contributor to productivity levels. There are some who claim that ecommerce is the driving force of economic success, making transportation a less critical component. Yet, America's transportation and logistics systems facilitate the growth of the ecommerce industry.

Most people still use transportation to either spend money or make money, both of which drive the economy. For this reason, transportation is a necessary input to economic activity. Therefore, it is important to understand which transportation investments will increase competitive business and are economically feasible.

However, transportation by itself will not solve all economic problems. It is not enough to believe that one road or one new rail or subway line will grow an area's economy. While transportation is a necessary contributor, it's not sufficient to help attract and retain jobs. Other critical factors—including a skilled labor force, developable land, and other supporting utilities—must be available to ensure a transportation project's success.

Strategically, transportation investments succeed in areas where transportation—or its lack—is an identified impediment to development. This is where investment can change behavior and where the measurement of economic development impact can help ensure a transportation project's higher probability of return in terms of productivity and competitiveness.

## EVALUATING THE AUTHOR'S ARGUMENTS:

**In this viewpoint Paula Dowell maintains that infrastructure has a benefit to the economy, business, and the public. Make an argument for increasing public transportation systems and infrastructure and how it could benefit your community.**

Viewpoint 2

# Transportation Infrastructure in the US Needs Help

*"Many of the highways and bridges built decades earlier are now reaching the end of their expected lifespan."*

## Steven J. Markovich

In the following viewpoint Steven J. Markovich maintains that transportation infrastructure in the United States and around much of the world is in terrifyingly bad shape. The author analyzes the problems with the costs of building and maintaining infrastructure and why some of the proposed solutions are not popular with the US public. Steven J. Markovich writes for a variety of publications, including the *Atlantic* and the Council on Foreign Relations' Renewing America blog.

### AS YOU READ, CONSIDER THE FOLLOWING QUESTIONS:

1. Who pays a large chunk of highway building and maintenance costs in the United States, according to the author?
2. According to statistics, what are the two top modes of public transportation?
3. Which countries work better at public-private partnerships, according to the viewpoint?

"Transportation Infrastructure: Moving America," by Steven J. Markovich, Council on Foreign Relations, October 14, 2014. Reprinted by permission.

Infrastructure is critical to economic growth, but the aging US transportation system suffers from insufficient investment. As this CFR Progress Report and Scorecard, Road to Nowhere, explains, other nations are building new highways as the United States' crumble. US transportation fell from fifth in the World Economic Forum's rankings in 2002 to twenty-fourth in 2011, passed by nations such as Spain, South Korea, and Oman. Making a U-turn will take some time since major infrastructure projects require several years to plan and execute.

The decline can be attributed to a general trend of under-investment in infrastructure; the American Society of Civil Engineers (ASCE) has only awarded overall grades of D or D+ to US infrastructure in all five report cards issued from 1998 to 2013. Current infrastructure requires more investment—for instance, one in nine US bridges are structurally deficient—while new projects are needed to address issues such as road congestion, which costs American drivers $101 billion annually in wasted time and fuel, and airport delays that are a $22 billion drag on the economy.

While experts have been warning about crumbling infrastructure for more than a decade, the federal government has not addressed underinvestment. The Obama administration has attempted to prioritize transportation infrastructure by making it the second largest component of the 2009 Recovery Act, and proposing the GROW AMERICA Act to provide four years of comprehensive funding to modernize highways, railways, and mass transit. But the former was a temporary measure and the latter is unlikely to gain traction in Congress. Aside from the Recovery Act and a two-year reauthorization plan passed in 2012, Congress has only passed short-term reauthorizations to keep the Highway Trust Fund afloat.

## Investing for Tomorrow

US transportation infrastructure requires substantial capital investment because many of the highways and bridges built decades earlier are now reaching the end of their expected lifespan. For the last few decades, the nation has benefited from investments from the Eisenhower era through the 1980s. From the 1980s onward, transportation infrastructure spending as a share of US GDP stagnated.

Experts generally agree that building infrastructure directly adds to short-term economic gains through the construction effort, and over the long term enables continued growth, though estimates of the level of return vary widely. There is also typical agreement that there are diminishing returns, and that other factors will affect how much of the potential gains will be realized.

Economists of the Federal Reserve Bank of San Francisco analyzed highway spending projects and localized economic growth and concluded that spikes in spending led to economic growth both immediately and in the medium term (six to eight years), but did not appear to accelerate growth beyond ten years. Standard and Poor's calculated that a $1.3 billion project will create an immediate real economic gain of $2 billion, with an unknown positive long-term effect. The World Economic Forum calculated a long-term gain of five to twenty-five cents on annual GDP for every dollar spent on public infrastructure. For private investors in Australia, it's estimated that infrastructure investments in the mid-1990s yielded 7 to 8 percent annually, with favorable risk exposure.

The entire world faces a large infrastructure challenge. McKinsey & Company estimates that the world will require $57 trillion in new infrastructure (including power, water, telecom, etc.) by 2030; global infrastructure spending was $4 trillion in 2012, but is expected to reach $9 trillion annually in 2025. Much of this funding may come from fuel taxes, which are substantially higher in OECD nations outside of North America. The investments made—or not made—today will shape not only next year's commute, but the ability of the US economy to effectively compete and grow decades hence, many experts say.

Falling construction costs have helped to put transportation infrastructure projects in reach for the United States. The Federal Highway Administration's (FHWA) National Construction Cost Index indicates that costs were elevated from 2005–2008, but have returned to historical norms. While previous FHWA reports found that highway funding was below the level required to just preserve the status quo, the 2013 report indicated that falling constructions costs allowed transportation investment to exceed replacement levels, but were still well short of making substantial improvement.

## Dwindling Trust Fund

Despite the recent fall in construction costs, public budgets are straining to fund projects. The federal government provides about half of funds used for building and maintaining highways, primarily from the Highway Trust Fund (HTF). While states and local governments provide three-quarters of all public spending on highways, 60 percent of that spending is for operations, while almost all federal spending is capital investment.

Even at current spending levels, the HTF no longer collects enough revenue to fund highway and mass-transit projects. HTF collects 18.4 cents of gasoline excise tax per gallon (and a tax on diesel as well), a nominal rate that has not changed since 1993, even as gasoline prices have shot up dramatically, and inflation has reduced the US dollar's value by a third; the real federal gas tax rate is at its lowest point since 1990. Rising fuel efficiency and recent declines in the average miles travelled have depressed HTF income even further; the efficiency of the average passenger vehicle has risen from twenty-four miles per gallon 1980 to thirty-six in 2013.

Funding uncertainty imperils coordinating construction efforts with state and local governments, and potential private partners. In 2008, HTF could not cover the costs of construction projects through its funds and needed an infusion from the US Treasury's general fund. A total of $54 billion has been transferred since 2008 to cover the gap.

The HTF needs more revenue—the Congressional Budget Office calculates a ten cent per gallon increase to make HTF solvent—but a hike is unpopular with the American public. In a 2011 poll by the Rockefeller Foundation, 66 percent indicated that improving transportation infrastructure was extremely or very important, but 71 percent said it was unacceptable to raise the federal gas tax rate, though large majorities supported alternative funding measures such as more private investment (78 percent) and creating a national infrastructure bank (60 percent).

Large majorities also were against new tolls, or moving to a vehicle-miles traveled (VMT) tax. VMT proponents argue that it would more directly tie to road use than the gas tax, and that revenues would not decline as cars get more efficient. VMT critics raise privacy and implementation concerns such as a need for an on-board system to report on mileage. Oregon is launching a pilot program for five thousand motorists in mid-2015.

## Mass Transit

Mass-transit capital spending on buses, trains, and subways is in worse shape than highway spending. The 2013 FHWA report indicates that even when including one-time Recovery Act funds, the $16.5 billion spent in 2010 on capital investments was below the $18.5 billion level to reach a good state of repair, let alone the $23.3 billion level to expand. Federal and local government combined to fund almost 87 percent of capital projects, with states covering the remainder. Public transportation is also widely subsidized; fares cover less than 38 percent of operating costs, with local and state governments making up most of the difference.

Approximately 7 percent of workers in the United States' one hundred largest metropolitan areas (6.5 million workers) rely upon mass transit to reach their jobs, but research by Brookings indicates considerable variability of access. On average, a resident can reach 30 percent of jobs in a metropolitan area via mass transit within ninety minutes, but that average masks a large discrepancy of access between urban (41 percent) and suburban (22 percent) job opportunities. Since higher skill jobs are more concentrated in cities, lower skilled workers typically have fewer mass-transit options. Most mass-transit trips are on a bus, with rail systems making up most of the rest.

Some high-profile large mass-transit projects are underway, such as a $5.6 billion project to link Washington, DC's metro to Dulles airport by 2018. The project is largely funded by the airport authority, but the federal government provided $900 million in direct funding, and a loan of $1.9 billion. It is a recent solution to a decades old problem—one common to many US cities—an airports many miles from downtown without a convenient mass-transit link.

Even without projects of that scale, cities could gain substantial leverage by better integrating existing mass-transit infrastructure to enable true door-to-door connections. Susan Zielinski of the University of Michigan recommends "New Mobility" hubs based on models deployed in Bremen, Germany that allow riders to seamlessly

## US Public Transportation Trips by Mode

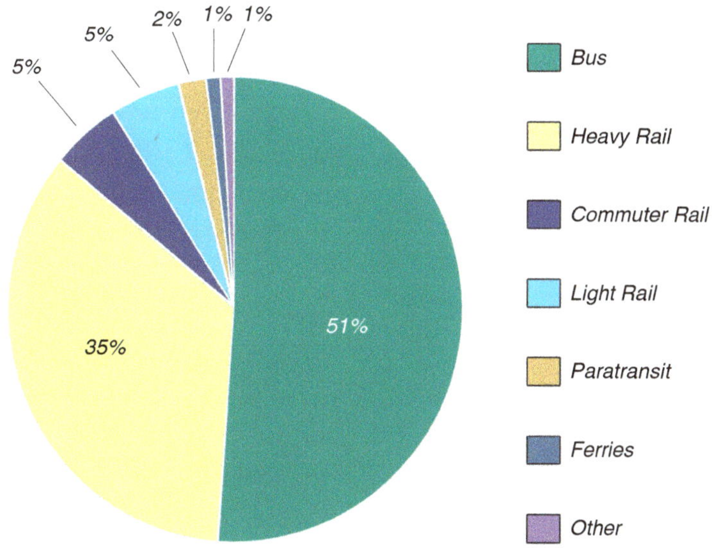


**Source: American Public Transportation Association**

*In the United States, buses are the most popular method of public transportation.*

transition between different transportation modes. These systems are aided by recent technological innovations such as smartphones that enable real-time schedule tracking or booking a car share and network-wide payment cards like London's Oyster Card.

The Obama administration has emphasized intercity high speed rail (HSR) projects since the Recovery Act, but so far, results have been disappointing. Multiple HSR projects have been cancelled by state governments, while new HSR lines exceeding two hundred miles per hour are being built in nations such as China, South Korea, Brazil, Saudi Arabia, and across Europe. While HSR could ease congestion at airports and on intercity highways, it is still unclear if they offer attractive returns. An analysis of high-speed rail by the Congressional Research Service found it rarely generates enough revenue to cover all capital and operating costs, particularly since the United States is less densely populated and has higher car ridership.

## Opportunity for the Private Sector

With traditional government-funded infrastructure investment in short supply, some policy experts are advocating for more

## Fast Fact

**In 2015, Pew Research Center found that 11 percent of Americans take public transportation on a daily or weekly basis.**

private-sector involvement through public-private partnerships (PPP). Through municipal bonds, private capital often helps fund infrastructure, but a PPP is a project with direct cooperation via long-term contracts between the public and private sector in development, construction, operation, ownership, or financing. PPPs are also more appealing to pension funds and foreign investors who cannot benefit from the tax deductibility of municipal bonds.

Ultimately, there is a different balance of risks and returns between private investors and the state, and how risk is shared can differ wildly from project to project. Greater private-sector involvement can sometimes bring significant technological or operational expertise that can result in lower costs compared to a public-sector led effort. Some states and municipalities already lease transportation infrastructure to private investors in long-term agreements, such as the ninety-nine-year lease for the Chicago Skyway bridge. The leases allow local governments to bring forward future toll revenue for reinvestment in other projects or to balance a budget while private investors obtain a stable revenue stream. Sometimes efforts are slow to mature. Launched with great fanfare in 2012, the Chicago Infrastructure Trust was part of a broader $7 billion infrastructure plan for the Windy City, but since then only one small energy efficiency project has gotten underway.

The United States has relatively limited but growing experience with PPPs compared to pioneers such as Canada, Australia, and the United Kingdom. Even as the private sector's role grows, governments will still be the prime actor for most infrastructure projects; successful PPP projects are often aided by national infrastructure offices that coordinate state and private action, such as PPP Canada, Infrastructure Australia, and Infrastructure UK. Not surprisingly, many of the largest infrastructure investors—including global leader Australia's Macquarie Group—are based in these nations.

CFR Senior Fellow Heidi Crebo-Rediker recommends that the federal government leverage its deep expertise by creating an advisory arm of the Treasury Department, "Infrastructure USA" to advise state and local governments in their efforts to leverage private capital to create public goods.

## EVALUATING THE AUTHOR'S ARGUMENTS:

**In this viewpoint Steven J. Markovich writes about the sad state of transportation infrastructure and the difficulties of trying to procure funding to improve the situation. Do you regularly use public transportation? Why or why not?**

Viewpoint 3

# "Transit Deserts" Strand People in Their Communities

*"In our car-loving society, people who cannot access transportation are excluded from their own communities and trapped inside 'transit deserts.'"*

## Junfeng Jiao and Nicole McGrath

In the following viewpoint Junfeng Jiao and Nicole McGrath maintain that "transit deserts" can cause serious problems for people in many cities. The authors argue that a majority of Americans use a car to get to work, but for certain groups of people this is simply not an option. Jiao and McGrath outline the patterns of transit deserts, the people who suffer from them, and the efforts being made to alleviate them. Junfeng Jiao is an assistant professor of community and regional planning and Nicole McGrath is an MS candidate of community and regional planning, both at University of Texas at Austin.

**AS YOU READ, CONSIDER THE FOLLOWING QUESTIONS:**

1. According to the viewpoint, what is a "transit desert?"
2. Which groups of people generally depend on public transportation as reported by the authors?
3. Where do "transit deserts" occur according to the authors?

"Stranded in Our Own Communities: Transit Deserts Make It Hard for People to Find Jobs and Stay Healthy," by Junfeng Jiao & Nicole McGrath, The Conversation, July 26, 2017. https://theconversation.com/stranded-in-our-own-communities-transit-deserts-make-it-hard-for-people-to-find-jobs-and-stay-healthy-77450. Licensed under CC BY-ND 4.0 International.

*Mass transit does not always reach low-income neighborhoods. If residents do not own cars, they can be cut off from access to job opportunities, services, and amenities.*

As any commuter who has experienced unreliable service or lives miles away from a bus stop will tell you, sometimes public transit isn't really a viable option, even in major cities.

In our car-loving society, where 85 percent of Americans use a car to get to work, people who cannot access transportation are excluded from their own communities and trapped inside "transit deserts." This term, which one of us (Junfeng Jiao) coined, describes areas in a city where demand for transit is high but supply is low.

Lack of transit has harmful effects on those who rely on public transit—generally, people who are too young, too old, too poor or have disabilities that don't allow them to drive. Mapping these deserts will help agencies adjust transit services and better serve their communities.

At UT Austin's Urban Information Lab, our research focuses on refining the methods used to quantify and measure transit supply and demand. We've developed clear and concise geographic information system (GIS) methods to evaluate transportation systems, providing alternatives to previous, more complicated network modeling. These methods can quickly be applied to any location, as we have shown in studies of five major cities in Texas and other cities across the United

States. By using this method, we found that hundreds of thousands of transit-dependent people in Texas don't have access to mass transit systems.

## Connecting People to Jobs and Services

Research shows that low-income residents living in sprawling areas have limited transportation options, which constrains their job opportunities and upward mobility. Inadequate transportation keeps people from finding work, which then reduces the productivity of their communities. It also can limit access to medical services, causing health problems to go undetected or worsen.

Addressing transit access is one important strategy for tackling broader social problems. For example, welfare recipients are less likely to own cars or have access to transit than the general population. Reducing these transportation barriers would help move them from welfare to work.

Although scholars have been studying "food deserts" (areas where residents lack access to nutritious food) for several decades, we have only recently applied this logic to mass transportation systems, despite the fact that food deserts often occur due to lack of transportation.

Relatively little research has been carried out to identify and quantify gaps between transit demand and supply. But as counties and cities feel the effects of declining funding from federal and state transportation user fees, they need new ways to target transportation infrastructure investments and ensure limited resources are used in the best way possible. We have found that maps are a promising way to guide these discussions.

## Mapping Transit Deserts

Determining exactly who relies on mass transit can be difficult. Existing information depends on census data. As previously noted, people who rely on transit are usually from marginalized demographic groups. They may be elderly, poor or have disabilities that keep them from driving. Census data do not account for the fact that sometimes these populations overlap (a transit-dependent person could be old as well as poor), so one individual could be counted many times.

Also, census data on car ownership are not available at the census block group level, which is the smallest geographic unit published by the US Census Bureau. This lack of data makes it hard to measure transit dependency with accuracy.

Measuring transit supply is easier. It relies on data from municipal planning agencies as well as relevant municipal and county GIS departments, which manage spatial and geographic information, analysis tools and mapping products. These agencies measure variables that include numbers of transit stops, transit routes and frequency of service, as well as lengths of sidewalks, bicycle lanes and low speed-limit routes (which are relevant because some commuters may opt to walk instead of taking the bus).

## Beyond City Centers

Current research shows that transit deserts exist all over the country. Cities such as Chicago; Cincinnati; Charlotte, North Carolina; Portland, Oregon; and San Antonio contain multiple communities that don't have enough transit services to meet existing demand. Even in older cities, where development tends to follow transit lines, there are neighborhoods where the supply of transit is simply not enough.

This is a large-scale problem. In San Antonio, the seventh-largest US city by population, some 334,530 people—nearly one-fourth of the population—need access to public transportation in a city that doesn't even have rail service. In Chicago, where there are high levels of transit dependency all across the city, just three of the transit desert neighborhoods that we identified house approximately 176,806 residents. Even in a city as progressive as Portland, Oregon, thousands live in transit desert neighborhoods.

When it comes to geographic location, transit demand and supply appear to follow certain spatial patterns. Unsurprisingly, transit supply is highest in city centers and decreases as distance from city centers increases. As a result, transit deserts do not typically occur in city centers or near downtown. In fact, because of the typical "hub and spoke" design of many transit services, city centers often have transit surpluses where supply outstrips demand.

The location of transit deserts often does not follow a geographic pattern, although they are usually associated with low-income and

## Fast Fact

**According to a Pew Research study, city dwellers in the Northeastern United States have the largest percentage of people using public transportation.**

remote areas. While planners and engineers may have a rough idea of where supply is low, making service adjustments requires measuring and mapping of transit supply and demand citywide.

## Rebalancing Transit Networks

Many cities are now making service adjustments to improve service to transit deserts. For example, Houston's transit authority, METRO, recently redesigned its bus service as part of a larger "Transit Service Reimagining," in an attempt to better meet the region's mobility needs. Evaluation of the new transit services shows that current levels of transit demand and supply are more balanced, though gaps still exist.

Identifying transit deserts is even catching on at the federal level. The US Department of Transportation recently launched a new initiative to map transit deserts nationally through a National Transit Map, which will put together data from different transit agencies into a complete feed. By accessing a larger, national look at transit demand and supply, regional agencies will have extra tools available to them when making changes to their local transit services.

What these changes will be is hard to say. Expanding existing bus services may be the most cost-effective way to improve transit access. Even in New York City, with its massive subway system, city officials are increasingly turning to bus rapid transit due to the high cost of adding new subway lines.

Adding bus lines, increasing service hours and even streamlining boarding and fares can help improve service and increase access. Integrating bicycling with transit services would be another cost-effective option.

As research on transit deserts continues to grow, more precise methods of quantifying the gap between transit supply and demand should develop. More research may provide new views on how the built environment and socioeconomic variables affect transportation accessibility. With careful planning and investment, these transit deserts can eventually transform into transit oases.

## EVALUATING THE AUTHOR'S ARGUMENTS:

**In this viewpoint Junfeng Jiao and Nicole McGrath analyze the issue of "transit deserts." Do you live in a transit desert? If so how does it affect your life? If not, how would you get around without a car or public transportation?**

Viewpoint 4

# Fixing Infrastructure Can Alleviate Inequality

*"A sudden infusion of infrastructure spending could benefit all Americans, creating good jobs and higher incomes for many."*

## Steven Pressman

In the following viewpoint Steven Pressman analyzes the poor quality of infrastructure against the backdrop of social inequality. Pressman contends that three areas are of most concern: water, roads, and rail. Besides highlighting the challenges, the author offers advice on how to correct the problems of infrastructure and demonstrates how these fixes will help solve inequality issues. Steven Pressman is a professor of economics at Colorado State University.

### AS YOU READ, CONSIDER THE FOLLOWING QUESTIONS:

1. What three types of infrastructure does the author believe should be improved?
2. According to the author, what should the top infrastructure priority be?
3. Why are bad roads particularly troublesome for poorer individuals, according to the viewpoint?

"3 Ways $2 Trillion for Infrastructure Can Fight Inequality Too," by Steven Pressman, The Conversation, February 5, 2019. https://theconversation.com/3-ways-2-trillion-for-infrastructure-can-fight-inequality-too-116393. Licensed under CC BY-ND 4.0 International.

Imagine you have US$2 trillion to spend on patching up America's crumbling roads, levees and other infrastructure. What would you fix first?

The nation's needs are great. The American Society of Civil Engineers' latest report, from 2017, highlighted derailing trains, roads full of potholes, levees breaching, bridges collapsing, undrinkable tap water and wastewater systems that are a menace to public health.

Choosing what gets funded—and what doesn't—may be a question US lawmakers will have to answer now that President Donald Trump, Speaker Nancy Pelosi and Senate Minority Leader Chuck Schumer have agreed to a very tentative $2 trillion infrastructure plan.

While it's still unclear where the money will come from, or how much they'll ultimately pony up, the more important question for me is where that money should go—and whom it should help. I believe three areas stand out: water, roads and rail.

## Infrastructure and Inequality

A sudden infusion of infrastructure spending could benefit all Americans, creating good jobs and higher incomes for many.

Decrepit infrastructure costs each US household an average of $3,400 every year due to productivity losses, higher transportation costs and other problems, according to the ASCE. That amounts to about $4 trillion in total over a decade, plus 2.5 million in lost jobs. It can also result in lost lives or severe health risks, such as when a bridge collapses or lead from an old pipe enters the water supply.

That's likely why the public overwhelmingly supports more spending on infrastructure—and why the deal between Trump and the Democrats finally came together.

But it's unclear whether Congress will ultimately agree to spend the promised $2 trillion—or even whether that'll be enough. So it's important to establish spending priorities.

Spending in areas that will help struggling working and middle-class families hurt by ever-rising economic inequality would be a good place to start. As research by myself and others has shown, inequality makes almost every aspect of human life worse, from infant mortality and crime to politics.

*Bad roads are a menace to the poor in particular. Found more often in low-income neighborhoods, potholes can cause severe and expensive damage to automobiles.*

## 1. The Water Crisis

That's why a top priority should be addressing the lack of potable water in many parts of the country.

Water is necessary for basic human survival. And unsafe water puts people's health and even their lives at risk. This has long-term consequences, especially for children. Furthermore, it reduces earnings and increases health care costs, which are ultimately paid for by everyone through lower tax collections and higher insurance premiums.

The ASCE report gave America's drinking water a D grade due to all the waste and risks from the nation's ancient, leaky and corroding piping system. And it's a problem that primarily afflicts poor communities, like Flint, Michigan.

Affluent communities usually have the political power to ensure safe drinking water and the money to pay slightly higher taxes for clean water if necessary. Low-income neighborhoods are usually neighborhoods with little political clout and will suffer most from water problems.

Low-income areas are also less able to cope with undrinkable water and afford the costs of replacing tap water with bottled water.

And people living in poor neighborhoods lack the ability to move, especially if they own homes that declined sharply in value because of water problem, as happened in Flint.

## Fast Fact

**According to the Federal Transit Administration, in 2013, 25 percent of rail transportation in the United States is in poor to marginal condition.**

## 2. Potholes and the Poor

Repairing America's crumbling road system is another urgent priority.

Roads, which also got a D grade from the ASCE, are increasingly falling into disrepair and becoming more dangerous for drivers. Again, the costs of the growing number of cracks and potholes fall most heavily on the poor—but they are also a burden for the middle class.

Bad roads mean an increased risk of car damage and more trips to the mechanic for expenses that easily can run into the thousands of dollars. Yet a recent Federal Reserve study found that 40% of Americans did not have even $400 to deal with an emergency expense.

An essential and unanticipated car repair could drain a savings account or be beyond someone's ability to pay. A high-interest loan from a payday lender could result in rates of well over 100% to consumers desperate for cash.

Or worst case, if repairs can't be paid for immediately, it might mean losing a job or dealing with lost income as a result of being absent from work. Poorer Americans typically have fewer vacation or personal days to use in such circumstances.

## 3. Bridging Divides with Rail

Railroads, which got the grade of D-, could also help reduce inequality that results from economic disparities among cities.

Many smaller cities have seen falling populations and declining incomes ever since the Great Recession, while larger metropolitan areas have thrived.

Although the causes of this growing divide are still unclear, improved rail service provides one potential solution.

For example, high-speed rail at affordable prices would make it easier for people living in medium-sized metropolitan areas like Akron and Canton, Ohio, to take jobs in larger cities like Cleveland that are not easily commutable at present. This would raise incomes for people living in these smaller cities and also increase the prices of their homes, where middle-class families store most of their wealth.

There are lots of ways to spend $2 trillion on infrastructure. Doing it in ways that help poorer and middle-income communities would put tax dollars where they are needed most.

## EVALUATING THE AUTHOR'S ARGUMENTS:

**In this viewpoint Steven Pressman highlights three areas of infrastructure that particularly need attention. Which of the three areas is most vital? Defend your argument with specifics from the viewpoint and also with content you've read in previous viewpoints.**

Viewpoint 5

# US Department of Transportation Funds Transportation Infrastructure

*"The [USDOT] is committed to revitalizing America's infrastructure using federal dollars as seed money."*

## US Department of Transportation

In the following viewpoint the US Department of Transportation (DOT) is shown to be invested in the future of America's infrastructure and committed to its funding. Individual projects and potential funding by the DOT are analyzed according to various infrastructure types. Established by Congress in October of 1966, the Department of Transportation aims to provide the United States with the safest transportation system in the world.

### AS YOU READ, CONSIDER THE FOLLOWING QUESTIONS:

1. How does the DOT work in partnership with states, according to the viewpoint?
2. What is one type of monetary program sponsored by the DOT?
3. In light of this viewpoint, which infrastructure projects would benefit working people?

"US DOT Provides More Than $63 Billion to Major Transportation Infrastructure Investments Across America in 2018," US Department of Transportation, October 10, 2018.

By the end of the 2018 fiscal year (FY 2018), the US Department of Transportation (USDOT) made available more than $63.9 billion in FY 2018 multi-modal discretionary and formula transportation investments and $1.6 billion in FY 2017 discretionary funds. This marks a significant step forward in funding the Administration's ambitious infrastructure goals.

The Department is committed to revitalizing America's infrastructure using federal dollars as seed money to encourage additional infrastructure investment by states, localities and private sector partners. Utilizing significantly increased levels of appropriations from Congress in the March 2018 omnibus funding bill, more investment is reaching areas and projects with the greatest impact.

Additionally, historic investment through DOT's programs in FY 2018 has begun to address the long-awaited infrastructure needs of rural communities, streamlined project delivery, and invested in transformative projects that benefit all Americans.

The Department has released Notices of Funding Opportunity (NOFOs) for nearly 90% of the funding from FY 2018 to solicit applications, and many have been closed or awarded. Overall, the Department has made an unprecedented infrastructure investment in America by making available more than $65.5 billion for key projects this year.

In just six months, the Department of Transportation has distributed the entire $56.2 billion in formula funds from FY 2018; announced $7.8 billion in discretionary grant availability from FY 2018; and awarded $5.8 billion in FY 2017 and FY 2018 discretionary grants to specific recipients.

Major grant programs including Infrastructure for Rebuilding America (INFRA), Better Utilizing Investments to Leverage Development (BUILD, (formerly Transportation Infrastructure Generating Economic Recovery, or TIGER)), and the Airport Improvement Program (AIP) are examples of DOT programs fulfilling these objectives. Highlights:

## BUILD Transportation Discretionary Grant Program

- In April 2018, the Department published a Notice of Funding Opportunity (NOFO) allowing applicants to apply for $1.5

*The condition of many US airports, particularly those that see the highest traffic, is dire. The DOT has committed to improving the safety and efficiency of these airports.*

billion in discretionary grant funding with a due date of July 18, 2018. This triples past funding provided for this flexible grant program focused on innovative projects that have significant local or regional impact.

- FY 2018 BUILD Transportation grants are for investments in surface transportation infrastructure and will be awarded on a competitive basis to projects with significant local or regional impact.

## Infrastructure for Rebuilding America (INFRA) Program

- In June 2018, the Department announced over $1.5 billion in proposed grants through the Infrastructure for Rebuilding America (INFRA) discretionary grant program. These proposed awards are from a NOFO that combined both fiscal years 2017 and 2018.
- These proposed awards will leverage an estimated $6.1 billion in additional funds from state, local and other funding sources. Together an estimated investment of over $7.6 billion

## Fast Fact

**The Department of Transportation began operations on April 1, 1967, after being enacted by Congress on October 15, 1966.**

will be spent on transportation infrastructure.

- INFRA grants will support the Administration's commitment to fixing our nation's crumbling infrastructure by creating opportunities for all levels of government and the private sector to fund infrastructure, using innovative approaches to improve the necessary processes for building significant projects, and increasing accountability for the projects that are built.

### Airport Improvement Program (AIP)

- The Airport Improvements Program provides funding for high-priority airport construction projects with an emphasis on maintaining and improving the safety and efficiency of the approximately 3,300 airports in the national airport system.
- Over $3 billion has been awarded to airports throughout the country. On September 27, Secretary Chao announced the first installment, $205 million, of an additional $1 billion in supplemental AIP funding provided by Congress.

### Transit

- In April 2018, the Department's Federal Transit Administration (FTA) announced approximately $264 million in project selections to improve the safety and reliability of America's bus systems and enhance mobility for transit riders across the country. A total of 139 projects in 52 states and territories will receive funding from FTA's Buses and Bus Facilities Infrastructure Investment Program.
- In June 2018, the FTA announced a NOFO soliciting applications under the Buses and Bus Facilities Infrastructure Investment Program for $366 million. Grant awards were made on September 25, 2018. The funds assist in the financing of buses and bus facilities capital projects, including replacing,

rehabilitating, purchasing or leasing buses or related equipment, and rehabilitating, purchasing, constructing or leasing bus-related facilities.

## Small Starts Grant Agreements:

- $56.2 million Laker Line BRT in Grand Rapids, MI (February 9, 2018)
- $16.9 million East Corridor First Coast Flyer BRT in Jacksonville, FL (March 7, 2018)
- $22.5 million for SMART commuter rail extension in San Rafael, CA (April 9, 2018)
- $43 million for Swift II BRT in Everett, WA (April 9, 2018)
- $29.9 million for Prospect MAX BRT in Kansas City, MO (April 9, 2018)
- $75 million for IndyGo BRT in Indianapolis, IN (May 15, 2018)
- $75 million for Tacoma Link inTacoma, WA (May 15, 2018)
- $75 million for Bus Rapid Transit in Albuquerque, NM (August 29, 2018)

## Rail

- The Department's Federal Railroad Administration (FRA) has issued Notices of Funding Opportunity (NOFOs) under the Consolidated Rail Infrastructure and Safety Improvements program totaling $568 million, of which $203 million for grants to support the implementation of Positive Train Control (PTC) were awarded on August 24, 2018. There is a further $343 million available for safety and infrastructure improvements.

## Pipelines and Hazardous Materials Safety Administration (PHMSA)

- In September 2018, PHMSA announced a total of $90 million in funding to states for pipeline safety and emergency preparedness. One highlight is the Hazardous Materials Emergency

Preparedness Grant program, totaling $22 million. This assists State and local governments, as well as Native American tribes, in safely and efficiently handling hazardous materials accidents and incidents. In addition, these funds will provide a comprehensive approach to emergency planning and training.

## Maritime Administration (MARAD)

- In June 2018, MARAD announced a NOFO soliciting applications under the America's Marine Highway Grants for $5 million. Grants were awarded on August 8, 2018. These grants support projects that are part of a designated Marine Highway project and will assist with mitigating landside congestion. In July 2018, MARAD awarded over $20 million in grants for Small Shipyards. These grants support capital improvements and increased efficiency. 29 shipyards received grant awards.

## Highways

- In addition to highways receiving major funding through the BUILD and INFRA programs, highway bridge projects can receive a share of a total $225 million in Competitive Highway Bridge Program (CHBP) grants, noticed on September 5, 2018.

### EVALUATING THE AUTHOR'S ARGUMENTS:

**In this viewpoint the DOT is shown as supporting the development of US infrastructure. Would Steven Pressman, the author of the previous viewpoint, agree with the plans put forth by the DOT? Why or why not?**

# Chapter 2

# How Does the Condition of Transportation Infrastructure Impact Society?

*Many of America's bridges and underpasses are patched up with temporary fixes.*

Viewpoint 1

# Urbanization Is Not Always Bad for the Environment

*"There are a number of reasons urbanization can be good for the environment, if managed properly."*

## Guanghua Wan

In the following viewpoint Guanghua Wan maintains that urbanization, though often maligned, can be a good thing. Urbanization often results from robust transportation infrastructure that allows people to move out from cities. Wan insists that urbanization that is properly managed benefits both people and the environment. Guanghua Wan directs research at the Asian Development Bank Institute.

**AS YOU READ, CONSIDER THE FOLLOWING QUESTIONS:**

1. What are three environmentally friendly ways that people use to get around in high density areas according to the viewpoint?
2. What is the link between urbanization and innovation?
3. How should cities be revitalized according to the author?

Urbanization degrades the environment, according to conventional wisdom. This view has led many developing countries to limit rural—urban migration and curb urban

"Urbanization Can Be Good for the Environment," by Guanghua Wan, Asian Development Bank, December 18, 2012. https://www.asiapathways-adbi.org/2012/12/urbanization-can-be-good-for-the-environment/. Licensed under CC BY-SA 3.0.

expansion. But this view is incorrect. There are a number of reasons urbanization can be good for the environment, if managed properly.

First, urbanization brings higher productivity because of its positive externalities and economies of scale. Asian urban productivity is more than 5.5 times that of rural areas. The same output can be produced using fewer resources with urban agglomeration than without. In this sense, urbanization reduces the ecological footprint. The service sector requires urbanization because it needs a concentration of clients. As services generally pollute less than manufacturing, this aspect of urbanization is also beneficial to the environment.

Second, for any given population, the high urban density is benign for the environment. The urban economics literature shows that compactness is a key determinant of energy use. High density can make public transport more viable and reduce the length of trips. Urban living encourages walking and cycling rather than driving.

Third, environment-friendly infrastructure and public services such as piped water, sanitation, and waste management are much easier and more economical to construct, maintain, and operate in an urban setting. Urbanization allows more people to have access to environment-friendly facilities and services at affordable prices.

Fourth, urbanization drives innovation, including green technologies. In the long term, environment-friendly equipment, machines, vehicles, and utilities will determine the future of the green economy. Green innovations in Asia's cities will be supported by the region's vast market as the billions of people who will be buying energy-efficient products will create opportunities and incentives for entrepreneurs to invest in developing such products.

Finally, the higher standard of living associated with urbanization provides people with better food, education, housing, and health care. Urban growth generates revenues that fund infrastructure projects, reducing congestion and improving public health. Urbanization fosters a pro-environment stance among property owners and the middle class, which is crucial for the introduction and enforcement of environmental laws and regulations.

Of course, urbanization also comes with costs. Millions of people are migrating to Asian cities and companies are locating there to employ them. Urban sprawl and industrial activities, such as power

*Reliable and accessible mass transit is an example of urbanization's positive effect on the environment.*

generation, transportation, construction, garbage and waste disposal, harm the environment. An assessment of the impact of urbanization on the environment must balance its benign and adverse effects. The Asian environment–urbanization relationship varies, depending on the level of development. Once a certain threshold has been reached, urbanization becomes good for the environment in terms of lower emissions of CO2 and particle pollution.

Cities in the 2000s enjoyed a better environment at the same level of urbanization than cities in the 1990s. To ensure green urbanization, developing countries need to continue the downward shift by adopting the following recommendations.

The first priority is to improve energy efficiency and conservation through appropriate pricing, regulations, and public sector support. It is vital to get prices right so that they incorporate the full social costs and benefits, and ensure the efficient allocation of resources. This can be done by imposing congestion and emission charges, as in Singapore, and by removing inefficient subsidies, as in Indonesia. Other examples are the introduction of carbon taxes, as in the Republic of Korea, and increasing block pricing for water, electricity, and other public utilities, as in the Philippines.

Countries need to introduce regulations and standards in a timely manner. These can correct for market or coordination failures on air, water, vehicles, and appliances, as in India. The government can build green industrial zones to attract manufacturing, as in Indonesia. Improved regulations can reduce or prevent urban sprawl.

## Fast Fact

**According to a United Nations report, by the year 2050, two-thirds of the world's population will live in urban areas.**

Cities need to build rapid public transport systems to improve connectivity and reduce pollution. Speedy connections to and from satellite cities can ease congestion in central megacity hubs. Rapid bus transit systems, as in the People's Republic of China (PRC), and subways, as in India, can reduce environmental degradation in densely populated cities and improve the quality of life.

The second priority is to promote renewable resources and new energy technologies. Waste-to-energy plants reduce pollution and generate energy, as in the Philippines and Thailand. Green technology can be acquired either by importation or innovation through research and development, as in the PRC.

The PRC is building new towns and satellite cities using renewable energy as primary energy sources. Urban sprawl can be tackled by reviving city centers and developing compact, walkable satellite cities centered on efficient train, light rail, or subway systems, without heavy reliance on highways and major roads.

The third priority is to help the poor by reducing disaster risks and improving slum conditions. Disaster risk reduction can be done by building dwellings in safe areas, improving housing affordability for the poor, and investing in drainage infrastructure and climate forecast technology. Policies to improve slum conditions include providing basic services, granting land titles to slum dwellers, and issuing housing vouchers linked in value to the length of a resident's tenure in the city.

The fourth priority is to strengthen public finance, transparency, and accountability. Public finance can be improved by broadening the tax and revenue base and by increasing the access of urban governments to broader and deeper capital markets in order to lower infrastructure and public service costs.

Politicians can be encouraged to do the right thing by disclosing city government performance to the public and nongovernment organizations, and having national competitions and campaigns to encourage a "race to the top" to reward high achievement.

## EVALUATING THE AUTHOR'S ARGUMENTS:

**In this viewpoint Guanghua Wan maintains that urbanization isn't necessarily always bad for the environment. Wan's examples in the viewpoint cite cases in Asian cities. Construct an argument showing how these ideas could work in US cities.**

Viewpoint 2

# Outward Spreading Urbanization Can Cause Problems

## Jillian Du and Anjali Mahendra

*"Failure to properly manage expanding land area exacerbates urban inequality and contributes to greater economic and environmental risk for the city."*

In the following viewpoint Jillian Du and Anjali Mahendra analyze a condition of many cities, that of outward expansion of urban areas. The authors report that this condition is trending in sub-Saharan Africa and South Asia. The authors highlight both the problems and challenges with this kind of development, as well as possible solutions. Jillian Du is a research analyst at the World Resources Institute and Anjali Mahendra is the director of research at the World Resources Institute.

**AS YOU READ, CONSIDER THE FOLLOWING QUESTIONS:**

1. As reported in the viewpoint, which three countries will account for major population growth between 2018 and 2050?
2. According to the authors, what three environmental problems occur with urban sprawl?
3. How are some cities already tackling urban sprawl problems?

"Too Many Cities Are Growing Out Rather than Up. 3 Reasons That's a Problem," by Jillian Du and Anjali Mahendra, World Resources Institute, January 31, 2019. https://www.wri.org/blog/2019/01/too-many-cities-are-growing-out-rather-3-reasons-s-problem. Licensed under CC BY-ND 4.0 International.

*Cities that expand outward can put a tremendous strain on natural resources and economies. In addition, inequality increases, with those living on the periphery paying more for accessibility and basic services.*

Imagine Lagos, Nigeria, a city of 22 million. What was once a small coastal town just a few decades ago has exploded into a sprawling megacity spanning 452 square miles. Its rapid growth has stretched the city's services impossibly thin: Less than 10 percent of people live in homes with sewer connections; less than 20 percent have access to tap water. Many houses are in slums and informal settlements at the city's periphery.

Now picture Lagos twice as big.

Lagos is one of many cities expected to grow exponentially over the next three decades, in both population and land area. Recent estimates show that urban land area could increase 80 percent globally between 2018 and 2030, assuming constant annual growth rates. When cities spread outward instead of upward, as Lagos has, it can worsen spatial inequalities and strain economies and natural resources.

In our new World Resources Report paper, Upward and Outward Growth: Managing Urban Expansion for More Equitable Cities in the Global South, we analyzed growth patterns for 499 cities using remote sensing. While cities growing vertically through taller buildings are located predominantly in wealthier cities in North America, Europe and East Asia, cities in sub-Saharan Africa and South Asia are growing mainly outward. These cities have the fewest financial resources to manage their growth but are expected to hold more than 2 billion additional people by 2050. As we know from the latest UN data, just three countries—India, China and Nigeria—are expected to account for 35 percent of global urban population growth between 2018 and 2050. As these cities grow in population, continuing their unwieldy expansion outward could push them into crises.

## Three Consequences of Unmanaged Urban Expansion

Failure to properly manage expanding land area not only exacerbates urban inequality, it also contributes to greater economic and environmental risk for the city as a whole. From Mumbai to Mexico City, it is all-too-common to see crowded slums grow larger and denser next to unaffordable, often vacant, high-rise developments. As municipal service networks fail to keep pace with urban growth, resource-constrained cities tend to react to development trends instead of having land development agencies proactively plan for growth.

Some of the implications of this unmanaged growth include:

### Greater Inequality

Like Lagos, many cities are already struggling with existing inequalities, inadequate service provision and stretched municipal capacities. Unmanaged land expansion exacerbates these struggles. Lower-income families typically move to a city's periphery in search of affordable housing. Yet the further they get from the city center, the more difficult their lives can become. Families at a city's edge will spend twice as much money and three times as much time commuting as families closer to jobs, schools and entertainment in the city center. As a city spreads outward, local agencies often struggle to provide water, sanitation and electricity. Citizens then have to rely on informal service provision—such as private water trucks and waste collectors that can charge up to 30 times more than city agencies—or go without these services, affecting their health and overall quality

**Fast Fact**

**According to a United Nations 2018 report, less than 50 percent of Africa's population is in urban areas.**

of life. Only the well-off can afford these coping strategies, leaving many urban residents underserved. Once these kinds of urban land development patterns begin, they have long-term effects on access to opportunities, productivity and quality of life.

## Economic Stresses for the City as a Whole

Research shows that as cities expand outward and population densities decline, the municipal costs of providing public services increase. In Indian and African cities, services like paved roads, drainage and piped water drop off sharply just 5 kilometers (3 miles) from the city. The associated investments for new infrastructure and social costs of their deficit only keep climbing as new urban areas are added. Moreover, sprawl means more congestion, pollution and longer commutes. Dirty air, mostly driven by heavy use of private cars and trucks, creates immense social and economic costs, such as health impacts and crop damage. In Chengdu, China, the economic loss from transport-related air pollution tallied $3 billion in 2013.

## Environmental Problems

Globally, the rate of urban land growth far outpaces population growth. This often comes at a cost to prime agricultural land, ecosystem services and biodiversity, which all contribute to food production and climate resilience. Already, we are seeing some of the fastest-growing urban areas in low-elevation coastal zones, flood plains, biodiversity hotspots and water-stressed areas. Rampant development in these sensitive ecosystems can further strain natural resources and lead to disastrous flooding from seasonal monsoons in many South Asian cities. Unregulated well-digging in cities such as Mexico City, Bangalore and Jakarta, which are growing outward rapidly and have little piped water and high water stress, is causing whole neighborhoods to sink. It's particularly troubling in Jakarta, where experts say that factoring in sea level rise, the city has only a decade to halt its sinking before millions of homes end up underwater.

## Reining in Unmanaged Expansion

These impacts are compounded by the fact that most outward growth currently underway in Africa and South Asia is unplanned and informal, or in locations where existing urban land use regulations do not apply. Some of this expansion is outside of cities' control, considering natural population increases and people migrating from rural to urban areas in search of economic opportunities. But other challenges are things cities can more proactively manage.

For example, distorted land markets can lead to speculative and fragmented development, where private landowners, real estate developers and corrupt public officials disproportionately benefit from rising land values. Weak planning, ineffective land-use regulations and certain market conditions are known to fuel expansion, relegating affordable housing to unserviced or poorly serviced locations at a city's periphery. And haphazard conversion of farmland and absorption of peripheral villages result in informal settlements or slums that are disconnected from city services.

Though a daunting challenge, some cities are already using innovative approaches to prioritize accessibility and manage urban expansion. Cities in Mexico, Brazil and South Africa are directing new development to already well-serviced and connected areas, instead of spreading outwards. Cities in Colombia, South Korea and India have been incrementally adding new land in well-connected and serviced locations by partnering with public utilities and private companies to help with financing. Many cities are also working with communities in informal settlements to create affordable density with more flexible planning standards and upgrading efforts.

The impacts of land-use policy changes in a city can last for many decades. Cities in Africa and Asia have a choice: Start managing unsustainable outward expansion today, or see problems worsen tomorrow.

## EVALUATING THE AUTHOR'S ARGUMENTS:

**In this viewpoint Jillian Du and Anjali Mahendra outline the ways that cities are presently dealing with urban sprawl resulting from transportation infrastructure. Compare and contrast the ideas presented in this viewpoint with the ideas presented by Guanghua Wan in the previous viewpoint.**

Viewpoint 3

*"Improving connectivity between and within countries can bridge stark differences in economic development by strengthening interregional trade."*

# Better Transportation Infrastructure Leads to Economic Gains and Reduction of Poverty

## Muneeza Mehmood Alam

In the following viewpoint Muneeza Mehmood Alam contends that better transportation infrastructure leads to improved lives through economic growth and alleviation of poverty. The author reports that improved transport infrastructure betters conditions in both rural and urban settings. These improvements can help alleviate inequality in urbanized areas of the world. Muneeza Mehmood Alam is an economist with the World Bank.

"Creating Pro-Poor Transport Connecting the Dots: Transport, Growth, and Poverty Reduction," by Muneeza Mehmood Alam, The World Bank Group, October 28, 2015. Reprinted by permission.

**AS YOU READ, CONSIDER THE FOLLOWING QUESTIONS:**

1. What are the mechanisms that reduce poverty through transportation infrastructure, according to the author?
2. Which modes of transport have helped countries in Africa?
3. How does poor public transport affect urban poor workers according to the viewpoint?

Transport plays a crucial role in connecting people to goods and services and fostering sustainable development. The literature links improved transport infrastructure to economic growth and poverty reduction through five key mechanisms (1) reducing transport and production costs, (2) creating jobs, (3) expanding productive capacity, (4) improving access to markets and basic services like health and education, and (5) reducing prices of final goods and services. These benefits depend on supportive conditions in other sectors, such as access to credit, functioning land markets, low trade barriers, and so on. Therefore, any assessment of potential gains from transport infrastructure and services should also account for the interaction with complementary markets. However, the analysis of such interactions—assessing how and when transport infrastructure can help reduce poverty and income inequality—is largely missing from the literature, leaving significant knowledge gaps across the spectrum of transportation settings. This note highlights existing findings and some limitations in the literature on three basic types of transport infrastructure: large projects such as regional or national highways and railroads; rural transport; and transport in urban areas.

## Regional and National Transit Corridors (Highways and Railroads)

Improving connectivity between and within countries can bridge stark differences in economic development by strengthening interregional trade. For example, five coastal countries in Africa—Angola, Kenya, Nigeria, South Africa, and Sudan—account for more than 70% of Africa's GDP. But in sub-Saharan Africa overall, estimates

*Tanzania's railroad network supplements the country's poor roads. The rail is a dependable way for those in rural areas to connect. Additionally, the train stops offer an opportunity for local merchants to sell their products to travelers.*

suggest that tightening the connectivity between cities by upgrading the primary road network can catalyze trade worth hundreds of billions of dollars.

In Peru, intercity highway upgrades increased the average annual rates of growth for exports (by 6%) and employment (by 5%). In China, connecting cities with railroads has moderately increased county-level GDP per capita, and in India, colonial railways boosted interregional trade and raised real income levels.

Improvements in transport infrastructure can also enhance firm efficiency and affect firm location. Upgrading highway infrastructure has allowed Indian firms to hold inventory for shorter durations, increased the survival rate of existing firms, and induced new firms to open near upgraded highways. In Indonesia, expressways have been associated with the dispersion of manufacturing activities.

## Rural Settings

Transport can play a crucial role in enhancing food security and agricultural productivity. For example, Africa could become self-sufficient in food and create a regional food market worth $1 trillion by 2030. But farmers will need better access to roads to trade their products. Africa's current food insufficiency is not surprising given the deficiencies in its road infrastructure—the average road density in low-income countries in sub-Saharan Africa is less than one-third that in other low-income countries. Improving rural road connectivity has been shown to increase agricultural productivity by reducing the travel time to agricultural markets, inducing farmers to adopt modern farming techniques and favor cash crops, and raising market participation. Improving road quality has also been shown to induce migration and shift workers from agriculture to manufacturing.

Research shows that reducing rural isolation—by lowering transportation costs and travel times or improving road access and proximity to markets— may have multiple benefits. It is associated with a reduced likelihood of a household's facing multidimensional poverty, with increased school enrollment rates for boys and girls and disadvantaged groups, and with greater use of distant hospitals.

## Urban Settings

> **FAST FACT**
> Africa's railroad infrastructure is difficult to improve because the continent is made up of 54 different governments, ministers of infrastructure, heads of state, and policies.

The placement of transport infrastructure within a city can alter the production mix of the urban economy, affect employment opportunities for the poor, and alter crime rates. For example, evidence suggests that the development of city roads in Colombia has shifted economic activity toward the production of lighter tradable goods. Similarly, transport infrastructure has altered the economic landscape of Chinese cities—radial highways have decentralized the services sector, radial railroads have decentralized the industrial sector, and ring roads have decentralized both sectors.

The urban poor rely heavily on public transportation for commuting. Without fast, secure, and affordable mass transportation, the urban poor are typically forced to walk to work, which is time consuming and limits their job search radius. Thus, the geographic dispersal of the labor market can dampen the gains from industrial agglomeration. A lack of security in the public transit system may also limit the labor market participation and job search radius of the poor, particularly for women, who are especially dependent on public transport. Even a simple intervention can make a difference: improving nighttime lighting reduced the incidence of crime around bus rapid transit stops in Colombia.

## Documenting the Poverty Dimension of Transport: A Long Way to Go

Documenting the link between transport interventions and the various dimensions of poverty and income inequality will require much more systematic attention from research. To date there is only limited evidence on the direct impact of transport infrastructure on poverty and income inequality. (1) For national transport infrastructure, improving interregional connectivity can enhance welfare by insuring farmers against bad weather. (2) Regarding rural settings, improvements in transport in Vietnam and Madagascar were most beneficial for the least developed and remotest areas. In contrast, in rural Nepal, easier access to roads appears to have benefited poor households but did not reduce income inequality. In rural Bangladesh, middle-income households benefited the most from investments in roads. (3) The impact of urban transport projects on the welfare of the poor is largely undocumented in the research.

## EVALUATING THE AUTHOR'S ARGUMENTS:

**In this viewpoint Muneeza Mehmood Alam reports that urban poor often have to walk to their jobs because of insufficient transportation. Do you walk to school, activities, or a job? If you had to, how would this impact your choices of schools, activities, or jobs?**

Viewpoint 4

# Transportation Infrastructure Has a Huge Impact on Public Health

*"Because the transportation system helps shape how communities are designed and operate, it can have a profound influence on public health."*

## Eloisa Raynault and Ed Christopher

In the following excerpted viewpoint Eloisa Raynault and Ed Christopher analyze the link between transportation and public health. The authors provide basic information how an active lifestyle improves health generally, and then give examples how various states and organizations are working to achieve better infrastructure to improve people's health. Eloisa Raynault is a program manager at the American Public Health Association and Ed Christopher is a community planner with the FHWA Resource Center.

**AS YOU READ, CONSIDER THE FOLLOWING QUESTIONS:**

1. As reported by the authors, how does "active transportation" benefit health?
2. What is one group of people that benefit from transportation infrastructure policies as mentioned in the viewpoint?
3. According to the authors, what is one way that Massachusetts has improved its transportation infrastructure policies?

"How Does Transportation Affect Public Health?" by Eloisa Raynault and Ed Christopher, US Department of Transportation, May/June 2013.

According to the Centers for Disease Control and Prevention (CDC), an estimated one in three adults and almost 17 percent of young people in this country are obese. Because the transportation system helps shape how communities are designed and operate, it can have a profound influence—both positive and negative—on public health.

The benefits of physical activity are well known: Exercise, including "active transportation" activities like walking and bicycling, can help prevent weight gain and lower the risks of obesity, diabetes, and heart disease. According to the US Department of Health and Human Services' 2008 Physical Activity Guidelines for Americans, "although some health benefits seem to begin with as little as 60 minutes (1 hour) a week, research shows that a total amount of 150 minutes (2 hours and 30 minutes) a week of moderate-intensity aerobic activity, such as brisk walking, consistently reduces the risk of many chronic diseases and other adverse health outcomes."

Where transportation infrastructure is designed to accommodate or even encourage nonmotorized transportation, such as through complete streets policies, it can have a positive effect on public health. In its research report, Planning Complete Streets for an Aging America, AARP notes that "the ability to live closer to daily destinations is an important factor in maintaining mobility among older people who cannot drive or whose driving is limited. People 65 and over living in areas where houses are built closer to shops and services are less likely to stay home on a given day, and are more likely to use public transportation and walk to get around."

The connections between public health and transportation are varied and well documented in peer-reviewed journals in both the public health and transportation arenas. A 2010 CDC study, for example, calculated that the costs of medical care and lost productivity associated with motor vehicle crashes exceeded $99 billion in 2005.

Another study, out of the University of California, Berkeley's Safe Transportation Research & Education Center, found significant health disparities in the area of transportation safety, with African-American, Native American, and Latino drivers facing higher traffic-related risks related to seatbelt use, impaired driving, and

*Cities with dedicated bicycle lanes contribute to overall improved health of their residents. Commuting by bike is not only good exercise, it is also better for the environment than cars and buses.*

pedestrian safety. Further, research has shown that limited access to transportation creates health inequities, as well as decreased access to education, employment, and opportunities for recreational activities for older adults and people with disabilities.

Transportation also is a source of pollution, generating air, soil, water, and noise pollutants, including particulate matter, carbon monoxide, nitrogen oxide, and carcinogens. Reports by the American Public Health Association and others have linked air pollution to negative health outcomes, including asthma, respiratory illness, heart disease, poor birth outcomes, cancer, and premature death.

To overcome these challenges, many in the transportation field are collaborating with colleagues in public health to research topics such as air pollution, safety, physical activity, and access to goods and services that support healthful living. This spotlight on public health and transportation complements other trends across the country, such as greater interest in alternative modes of transportation, livable communities, and resource conservation.

Complete streets and land use strategies that consider health can help increase physical activity, improve accessibility and safety, and ease congestion and air pollution. "As the use of these strategies increases," says Andrew Dannenberg, an affiliate professor at the University of Washington's School of Public Health, "there is tremendous potential for studying how health outcomes may be improved via transportation."

[...]

## Public Health on The MPO Front

MPOs are federally mandated bodies for urban areas larger than 50,000 people and are responsible for the transportation planning for their areas. By law, MPOs serving urbanized areas with more than 200,000 people must have policy boards composed of local elected officials, State department of transportation (DOT) representatives, and the providers of major modes of transportation, including transit services and airports. All MPOs must have policy boards that include local elected officials. MPOs decide how Federal transportation funds for their areas will be spent, thus playing a major role in setting transportation policy and approving different types of transportation facilities.

Many MPOs are becoming concerned about the effects of their plans and programs on public health. Regional plans like the one published in 2010 by the Chicago Metropolitan Agency for Planning now call for "pursuing opportunities for more compact, walkable, and mixed-use development," and making "significant, criteria-based investments in parks and open space" as a means to achieve "major benefits . . . including enhanced quality of life" and "improved public health through the promotion of active lifestyles."

Around the country there are countless examples of MPOs explicitly incorporating public health into their planning, policy, and project selection processes. In a December 2012 report, Metropolitan Area Transportation Planning for Healthy Communities, the Federal Highway Administration (FHWA) documented the efforts of four MPOs—those in Nashville, TN; Seattle, WA; Sacramento, CA; and San Diego, CA—that are successfully considering aspects of health during the transportation planning process. What follows are highlights from that report, as well as a summary of similar efforts in San

Francisco, CA, and in a Midwestern region known as the Quad Cities, which includes cities in Illinois and Iowa along the Mississippi River.

[...]

## Public Health at the State Level

In addition to health-related activities at the MPO level, many States are taking steps to consider the health effects of transportation in the planning process. Some notable efforts are underway in Massachusetts, Minnesota, and North Carolina.

In June 2009, State legislators signed into law the Massachusetts Healthy Transportation Compact, which put in place an interagency initiative to facilitate transportation decisions that balance the needs of all transportation users, expand mobility, improve public health, support a cleaner environment, and create stronger communities. The State's secretaries of transportation and health and human services cochair the compact, which also includes the secretary of energy and environmental affairs, the Massachusetts Department of Transportation's (MassDOT) high-way administrator, the MassDOT transit administrator, and the commissioner of public health. To achieve the com-pact's goals, the department is forming partnerships with the public and private sectors, advocacy groups, and transportation, land use, and public health stakeholders.

"What is key is that these partnerships are breaking down traditional policy silos and inspiring innovation at all levels to advance healthy transportation outcomes," says Catherine Cagle, MassDOT's manager of sustainable transportation.

In October 2012, MassDOT Secretary Richard Davey announced a statewide goal of tripling the share of travel in Massachusetts by bicycling, transit, and walking, further affirming the State's interest in promoting active transportation.

[...]

## FHWA Working Group

To complement efforts at the local and State levels, FHWA established an in-house working group in January 2012 consisting of staff representing 11 offices. The group's purpose is to explore how the agency

**FAST FACT**

**Portland, Oregon; Washington, DC; and Minneapolis, Minnesota, are the top cities in the United States for bike commuters.**

addresses health-related issues and requests for information. Although FHWA has no formal policy on health, agency officials recognize that public health is an integral part of transportation planning and program delivery and should be considered as part of decision-making in the public interest.

During its first year, the working group's accomplishments included defining health in transportation, identifying FHWA programs related to health, and developing an annotated bibliography of health-related resources. The group also created a health response team charged with responding to inquiries from State and local agencies.

An informal survey of planners at FHWA division offices in 2012 indicated that the agency is handling a number of questions on health-related topics:

- Considering public health in the long-range transportation planning process
- Reducing the severity and number of obesity cases through more walkable communities, complete streets, and livability goals
- Understanding health impact assessments
- Identifying infrastructure that supports or hinders transportation to human services
- Addressing urban food "deserts"
- Measuring response times for emergency medical services in congested corridors
- Assessing crash survivability in smaller electric or energy-efficient cars

In addition, FHWA's Office of Planning, Environment, and Real Estate recently launched a "Health in Transportation" section on its Web site and will soon offer answers to frequently asked questions, as well as links to related publications and training opportunities.

In its second year, the working group will coordinate its activities with the Office of the Secretary of Transportation, the Federal

Transit Administration, and the National Highway Traffic Safety Administration, all of which hold a stake and interest in protecting public health.

"The working group has done an effective job compiling health in transportation information and improving their competency to provide technical assistance to the field," says Associate Administrator Gloria Shepherd, of FHWA's Office of Planning, Environment, and Real Estate. "We hope to advance the state of the practice by compiling and sharing this type of information with the MPOs and State DOTs as they consider it in the planning process."

## EVALUATING THE AUTHOR'S ARGUMENTS:

**In this viewpoint Eloisa Raynault and Ed Christopher write about the connection between physical activity and transportation and how organizations are trying to improve active alternatives to getting around. How often do you ride a bike for pleasure or purpose—such as getting to school or work or to run errands?**

Viewpoint 5

# Bridge Collapses Can Claim Lives and Impact Economies

*"To an engineer, failure and collapse have different meanings."*

## James Brownjohn

In the following viewpoint, James Brownjohn analyzes why bridges collapse, and how engineers might prevent such collapses from happening. The author explains the various causes that can lead to the collapse or failure of bridges. Finally, the author examines ways that bridges might be made safer in the future. James Brownjohn is a professor at the University of Exeter in the United Kingdom specializing in structural dynamics.

### AS YOU READ, CONSIDER THE FOLLOWING QUESTIONS:

1. As stated by the viewpoint, what are two main reasons that bridges collapse?
2. What is the difference between a bridge collapse and a bridge failure as explained in the viewpoint?
3. According to the author will technology replace human inspection of bridges?

"Explainer: Why Do Bridges Collapse?" by James Brownjohn, The Conversation, May 28, 2013. https://theconversation.com/explainer-why-do-bridges-collapse-14653. Licensed under CC BY-ND 4.0 International.

*The MacArthur Maze overpass connecting to the San Francisco–Oakland Bay Bridge collapsed when a gasoline truck overturned and burst into flames. The heat from the fire weakened the road's steel beams.*

Bridge collapses are often tragic but are also fascinating for bridge engineers as they usually provide puzzles to solve and often lead to major changes in design, construction and management.

Complete bridge collapses, such as the highway bridge that collapsed in Washington State last week and the Minneapolis I35 West Bridge in 2007, are relatively rare.

The cause of the Washington bridge collapse is obvious; an oversize truck collided with critical structural elements. Others, like I35W, the Tacoma Narrows Bridge (the famous Galloping Gertie, also in Washington State) that broke apart during normal wind conditions, and Palau Bridge, require significant detective skills as advanced as those used in aircraft crash investigations.

## Design Flaws

I35W collapsed because of overloading during construction and the faulty design of a small but critical structural component. Galloping Gertie collapsed because of trends towards efficient design of North American long-span bridges and because memories of similar wind-driven collapses in Europe and USA had become too distant. Palau Bridge also appears to have collapsed due to inadequate design.

Other reasons for total collapse include vehicle overload, scour and collapse of bridge piers, metal corrosion and fatigue, defective material (increasingly rare), impact by a vehicle as in this most recent case, neglect and general deterioration.

In the distant past footbridges have been destroyed by pedestrian action for example soldiers marching in step, but this is a well understood problem these days and the worst case result is embarrassment and litigation.

## Natural Causes

There are also well known examples of bridge collapse due to flooding (for example in Cumbria in 2009), earthquakes, and very rarely these days due to excessive winds.

Design codes engineers need to follow (by law or otherwise) prescribe "actions" specific to location, such as maximum credible earthquake and wind speed. Designs must take these actions into account in combination with other more common forms of loading (for example from vehicles and or due to temperature).

> **Fast Fact**
> According to the American Society of Civil Engineers, in 2016, 9.1 percent of the bridges in America were structurally deficient.

Bridges still collapse during earthquakes because older designs missed out on important new understandings about the way structures work in earthquakes and have not been upgraded. And by their very nature earthquakes are random events; history does not provide enough information to assess precise seismic hazard everywhere structures are built, so we learn by (painful) experience.

But we learn directly from earthquake-induced failures. Causes of bridge collapse during earthquakes are studied by forensic structural engineers from around the world through post-earthquake missions.

As well as bridges in operation, there have also been many cases of bridge collapse during construction, such as at Kota, India in 2008. The causes of these collapses are more complex, due to the timing and interaction of the various construction methods and the increased possibility for human error.

## The Element of Surprise

It is also worth remembering that to an engineer, failure and collapse have different meanings. The London Millennium Bridge did not collapse, but it still failed. It was not fit for purpose until a costly retrofit made it immune to the lateral forces generated by pedestrian crowds.

Structural trauma caused by earthquakes, floods and fire may not result in total collapse but can seriously damage or weaken a bridge.

Other problems may be less obviously destructive and come with the element of surprise discovery. Corrosion is a major threat to bridges. It led to the closure of Hammersmith flyover at a critical time before the London 2012 Olympics.

With a bridge still standing and even in restricted operation, assessing its condition under conflicting requirements for safety and minimising disruption can provide greater challenges for structural engineers than for bridges that have completely collapsed.

## Keeping Bridges Up

So how can engineers prevent bridge collapse, and how can engineers know if a bridge has deteriorated or suffered damage that compromises safety of users?

These are two rather different issues. In the first case, design codes and safety factors provide comfort zones in which engineers can operate. When designs become clever (for example Tacoma Narrows and the London Millennium Bridge) factors that have worked to keep simpler designs safe may be lost.

Our experience of different types of loading (for example from winds or earthquake) is constantly enhanced. Design guidance is constantly revised and risk is reduced. In cases of exceptional landmark structures, experimental studies on sophisticated models may be carried out using laboratory tools such as wind tunnels, shaking tables and centrifuges, further reducing the possibility for surprise.

With modern methodologies and safe working requirements, construction accidents are increasingly rare in developed countries. However with realistic economic constraints it is all but impossible to guard against "low probability, high impact" events such as terrorism, freak vehicle accidents and weather.

For structures that age, deteriorate and have to carry ever increasing loads, and in the case of bridges that have partially failed or been damaged due to trauma, there are emerging technologies to assist engineers in a similar way to medical diagnostics.

Researchers worldwide and agencies such as US Federal Highway Administration are taking steps to develop technologies that improve the way engineers manage bridges to maintain safety, reduce costs and cope with increased demand.

This technology is only being adopted very slowly, but there are some striking examples in major long span structures throughout the world.

Forth Replacement Crossing in Scotland will have a highly sophisticated performance and health monitoring system based on designs that have been in operation in Hong Kong for more than a decade.

Such systems are largely intended to check whether structures are behaving (performing) as designers intended.

There is still a long way to go before such technologies can replace manual inspections and the skills and efforts of bridge maintenance engineers, but exciting developments in sensors and data interpretation technology show great promise.

## EVALUATING THE AUTHOR'S ARGUMENTS:

**In this viewpoint James Brownjohn provides a balanced viewpoint which analyzes how bridges collapse and what might be done to prevent this tragedy. If you were in charge of funding infrastructure repair, how would you collect money for this?**

Viewpoint 6

# Saving Lives Is a Goal of Transportation Infrastructure

*"Projects that reduce traffic and improve infrastructure can have a positive impact on traffic safety."*

Claudia Adriazola-Steil and Nicolae Duduta

In the following viewpoint Claudia Adriazola-Steil and Nicolae Duduta maintain that safety issues should not be overlooked when transportation systems are improved. The authors highlight the increased safety impacts of rapid transit bus systems and the efforts of some major world cities to improve conditions for cycling. Claudia Adriazola-Steil is the director of health and road safety for World Resources Institute and Nicolae Duduta previously was on staff at WRI.

**AS YOU READ, CONSIDER THE FOLLOWING QUESTIONS:**

1. Where have bus rapid transit systems become safer?
2. Which cities have made cycling safer, as stated in the viewpoint?
3. How many people die in traffic crashes each year?

Sustainable transport initiatives have gained traction in recent years in developing world cities. This trend can be seen in the growth in Bus Rapid Transit and Busway systems around the

"Saving Lives with Sustainable Transport," by Claudia Adriazola-Steil and Nicolae Duduta, World Resources Institute, May 12, 2013. https://www.wri.org/blog/2013/12/saving-lives-sustainable-transport. Licensed under CC BY-ND 4.0 International.

world, the new bike-sharing scheme in Mexico City, or the investment in cycling networks in Turkish cities, to name just a few examples. However, these types of initiatives often overlook what should be a key component in their planning—traffic safety. While sustainable transport initiatives are usually proposed and evaluated based on their impact on travel times, local air quality, accessibility, or greenhouse gas (GHG) emissions, their potential traffic safety impacts are often overlooked.

A new publication from EMBARQ highlights this issue, exploring the existing literature on the safety impacts of sustainable transport—primarily from the United States and Europe—and adding examples from Latin America and South Asia. The evidence suggests that projects that reduce traffic—such as congestion charging—and those that improve infrastructure—such as high-quality mass transport systems—can have a positive impact on traffic safety, in addition to numerous other co-benefits.

## Safety Impacts of Mass Transport

Take the TransMilenio bus rapid transit (BRT) system in Bogotá, Colombia. This BRT system is often hailed as an innovative model for mass transport, particularly among cities in the developing world. In addition to its well-documented impacts on reducing greenhouse gas emissions and travel times, the first TransMilenio corridor on Avendia Caracas has had an equally significant though under-acknowledged role in improving traffic safety. Findings show that the BRT has contributed to an estimated 50 percent reduction in traffic fatalities on the avenue, helping avoid more than 200 traffic deaths during its first nine years of operation.

The TransMilenio is not the only BRT system that has dramatically improved traffic safety. BRT and other transit priority projects in Guadalajara, Mexico; Mexico City; Ahmedabad, India; and Melbourne, Australia have similarly curbed traffic crashes and fatalities, while improving the quality of transport in their respective cities. The improved safety record is due mainly to the changes in street infrastructure typically needed to accommodate a BRT—such as creating a central median, making crosswalks shorter, and reducing the number of mixed traffic lanes—all of which tend to contribute to fewer crashes.

*Bogotá's TransMilenio BRT system has contributed to a reduction in greenhouse gas emissions and successfully alleviated the number of traffic fatalities.*

## Active Transport and Traffic Safety

Cities that have implemented policy and infrastructure to promote cycling have also seen significant safety benefits. Copenhagen and New York City, for example, have both invested in creating or expanding citywide networks of dedicated bike lanes and tracks to promote cycling. In Copenhagen, the total volume of cycling has increased by 28 percent between 1998 and 2009, while the rate of injuries and fatalities to cyclists has decreased by 53 percent. Similarly, New York City had four times as many bicycle commuters in 2010 as it did in 2000, while the city's cycling injury rate (the ratio of cycling injuries to cyclist commuters) declined by more than 70 percent.

It also appears that the safety benefits of cycle infrastructure are not limited to cyclists. A study in New York City found that streets with bike lanes are also safer for pedestrians, a finding that could be attributed to the reduced traffic speeds associated with the introduction of bike lanes and tracks. New York City has also taken key steps to improve walkability and pedestrian infrastructure, with significant benefits for pedestrian safety.

## Implications for Cities in the Developing World

**FAST FACT**

**According to the National Highway Traffic Safety Administration, in 2015, 35,092 people died in car crashes on US roadways.**

Traffic crashes currently claim more than 1.2 million lives every year, according to the World Health Organization (WHO). That number is increasing, particularly in low and middle-income countries.

In an effort to raise awareness about traffic safety issues and encourage local and national governments to focus on reducing traffic crashes and fatalities, the United Nations declared 2011 to 2020 as the Decade of Action on Road Safety. The initiative includes a clear focus on safe mobility and sustainable urban transport. The WHO has also recognized the importance of sustainable transport in achieving the ambitious goals of the Decade of Action. Its latest Global Status Report on Road Safety includes policies to promote walking and cycling and investment in mass transport as critical safety indicators for countries.

Recognizing the potential safety benefits of sustainable transport is a key step, but it is also important to ensure that this translates into high-quality projects on the ground. Through innovative policies and sustainable transport projects, cities in developing countries can meet their growing mobility needs while also significantly improving safety.

### EVALUATING THE AUTHOR'S ARGUMENTS:

**In this viewpoint Claudia Adriazola-Steil and Nicolae Duduta analyze the issue of safety in transportation. Compare their views with the views of Eloisa Raynault and Ed Christopher from a previous viewpoint in this chapter.**

# Chapter 3

# How Should Transportation Infrastructure Be Changed?

*Will the transportation infrastructure of the future look completely different?*

Viewpoint 1

# Fully Automated Vehicles Will Revolutionize Urban Transportation

*"Theoretically we could satisfy the mobility demand of a city with only a small fraction of the cars we have today."*

## Carlo Ratti

In the following viewpoint Carlo Ratti offers a vision of the future of transportation in urban areas. Ratti argues that, for one thing, car sharing will reshape our roads, as an excess of cars, which end up being stationary much of the time, hampers mobility. Fully automated cars won't sit unused in parking garages or at our homes; they can ferry one family member to work, then return home and drive another to school. In that way, carsharing can mimic public transportation. Carlo Ratti is professor of urban technologies and planning at Massachusetts Institute of Technology and the director of the SENSEable City Lab.

"How Intelligent Will Future Transportation Be? by Carlo Ratti, Director of the Senseable City Lab at MIT and founding partner of Carlo Ratti Associati design and innovation practice in New York and Turin. Reprinted by permission.

**AS YOU READ, CONSIDER THE FOLLOWING QUESTIONS:**

1. How will traffic be monitored in the author's "Smart Roads" project in Italy?
2. How could autonomous vehicles impact the use of public transportation?
3. Can we look forward to riding in flying cars, according to the viewpoint?

How will future transportation change our cities? Flying cars are not likely says Carlo Ratti, architect and engineer. Urban mobility will be revolutionized to a greater extent by car sharing, autonomous vehicles and smart roads.

"For 95 percent of the time, private vehicles are stationary in parking lots, traffic jams, and even parked at people's homes," is how Carlo Ratti describes the inefficient state of worldwide car usage. The engineer, architect and director of the "Senseable City Lab" at the Massachusetts Institute of Technology (MIT) feels the solution lies in car sharing concepts whose importance will increase exponentially with the growing number of automated vehicles: "Sharing a car can replace ten to 30 others." Among other things, Ratti deals with the question of how future transportation systems will change urban life. "Theoretically we could satisfy the mobility demand of a city with only a small fraction of the cars we have today."

## Sustainable Transportation Concept

According to Ratti, fully automated vehicles will revolutionize urban transportation: "They will dissolve the divide between private and public transportation. 'Your' car can drive you to work in the morning and then family members or somebody from your social media community can use it for the rest of the day."

Carsharing and autonomous vehicles could mean fewer cars and therefore more space that could be put to other uses. Not only on the roads: "For every car in the United States, there are approximately three parking spaces—not including the private ones in front of houses. All in all, it totals about 13,000 square kilometers, which

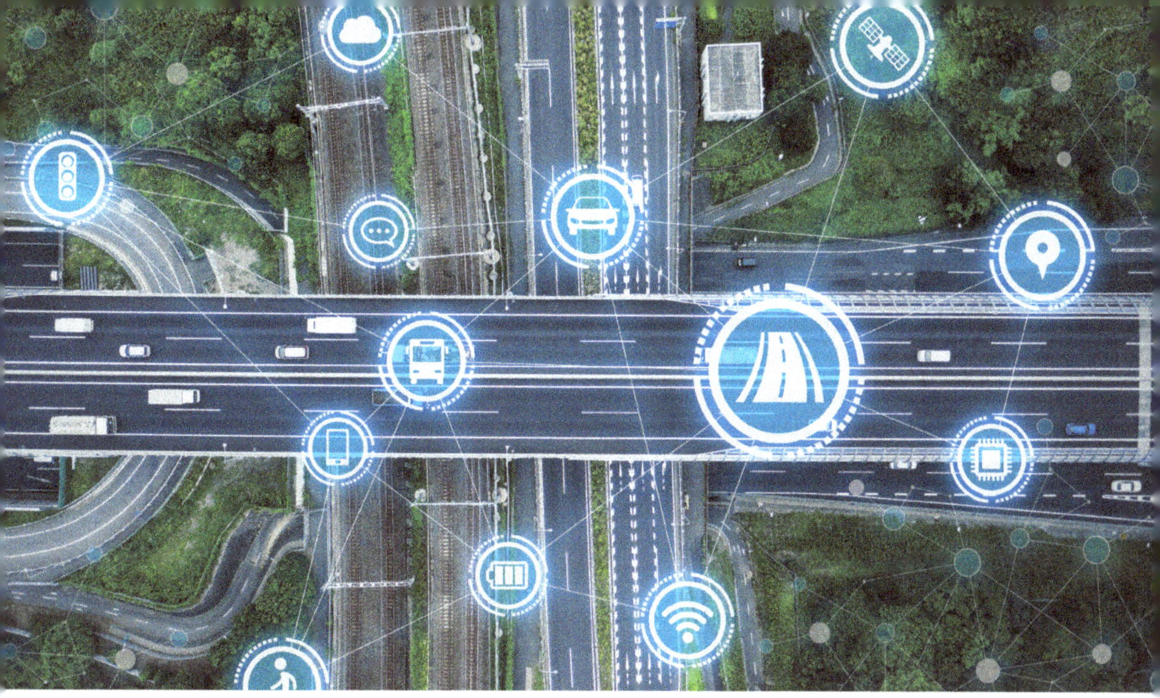

*Plans for roads of the future focus on the incorporation of technology.*

corresponds to an area bigger than Puerto Rico." This space could be used for playgrounds or urban gardening—creativity knows no bounds when converting such free spaces.

## Internet of Roads

That roads will also soon start to "think" is something made obvious by the "Smart Roads" project that is to be implemented on over 2,500 kilometers of roads in Italy. It has been developed together by the Italian infrastructure company ANAS and Carlo Ratti's design and innovation practice Carlo Ratti Associati. "The aim is to improve traffic management and safety conditions on the roads. We want to place a digital layer over the existing physical infrastructure of the road network to exchange big data efficiently," explains Ratti.

On these smart roads, drones will monitor traffic as well as the immediate surroundings, and in an emergency they can fly first aid kits to an accident. In doing so, they receive help from intelligent poles that serve the drones as charging stations, bundle their information and record environmental data like air pollution, wind speed or weather changes. These are then transmitted to smartphones or on-board navigation systems belonging to today's drivers and the

**FAST FACT**

**According to Pew Research, in 2014, 44 percent of Americans want to drive in autonomous cars versus 56 percent who would not.**

autonomous vehicles of tomorrow. They also provide drivers in real time with personalized information about for instance the traffic situation or upcoming road conditions. The next step on the way to an "Internet of Roads" scenario will be to link this data with information collected by the vehicles themselves. A wi-fi system integrated within the poles ensures that everybody travelling on the road stays online.

## Becoming More Flexible

According to Ratti, infrastructure will not undergo any essential changes. What on the other hand will dramatically change is urban areas and life: "The digital and physical world will merge—a totally new experience of the city." It is all about flexibility and user orientation. Ratti cites the "Dynamic Street" project as a current example—a prototype that Ratti and his colleagues have developed with Sidewalk Labs, a start-up belonging to the Google parent company Alphabet.

The dynamic street adapts to its users in real time thanks to an IoT system: "A street where automated cars drive in the morning, children play in the afternoon, and which becomes a baseketball court on the weekend," is how Ratti describes the concept. Light signals serve as markings for parking spaces or traffic lanes. This way an additional lane can be added for example during rush hour and then disappears in the evening.

## A Question of Funding

The new technologies come with challenges: "Autonomous vehicles could lead to an unfair competitive advantage. The cost of traveling a mile might sink to such a degree that people will abandon public transportation in favor of self-driving cars." The result would be more cars back on our streets and roads.

Relief could come in the form of a tax on individual mobility and subsidies for public transport. It however raises complex funding issues: “I see dynamic road pricing systems like those in Singapore as a possible source of income,” explains Ratti. It would mean pay stations in areas with heavy traffic. With integrated chips in vehicles, drivers would pay a toll that varies depending on the time of day and traffic. The results are positive—less traffic jams and a more efficient utilization of roads. In general, Ratti stresses that one should not only rely on cars but efficiently combine various means of transportation—like e-scooter services, public transport or e-bike sharing.

## Don’t Take Off

However, “air taxis” or “flying cars” play no role in Ratti’s vision: “They are to be seen in films like Metropolis or Blade Runner and are in the imaginations of investors but I think that, even now, cars on roads are dangerous. Just imagine what it’d be like in the air. In my opinion, we should stay firmly on the ground when it comes to transport.”

## Summary

According to Carlo Ratti, the city of the future is flexible and adapts itself to its inhabitants thanks to big data. He is convinced that when the digital and physical worlds merge, it can revolutionize urban transportation, dissolve infrastructure issues and increase quality of life.

### EVALUATING THE AUTHOR’S ARGUMENTS:

**In this viewpoint Carlo Ratti advocates autonomous vehicles and car sharing. How would this differ from public transportation? Do you think Americans would embrace it? Why or why not?**

Viewpoint 2

# For Many Reasons, Public Transportation Should Be Expanded

*"Air pollution from motor vehicles continues to contribute to adverse respiratory and cardiovascular health effects."*

## US Department of Health & Human Services

In the following viewpoint the US Department of Health & Human Services provides a balanced outlook on the expansion of public transportation in the United States and the benefits that would result from such an expansion. Many positive effects are known to occur with an increased availability of this type of transportation, which deemphasizes the role of automobiles. The US Department of Health & Human Services is a governmental agency of the United States.

**AS YOU READ, CONSIDER THE FOLLOWING QUESTIONS:**

1. Which populations of individuals benefit from public transportation according to the viewpoint?
2. What type of vehicle is favored by today's transportation infrastructure?
3. How are health benefits improved with better public transportation as stated in the viewpoint?

"Public Transportation System: Introduction or Expansion," US Department of Health & Human Services.

*Municipal buses allow citizens with disabilities and mobility issues to retain their independence.*

Public transportation systems include a variety of transit options such as buses, light rail, and subways. These systems are available to the general public, may require a fare, and run at scheduled times. The purpose of introducing or expanding public transportation is to increase access to and use of public transit while, at the same time, reducing motor vehicle miles driven and traffic congestion.

Public transportation systems are often implemented at the local or regional level and can be supported by federal initiatives, such as the Fixing America's Surface Transportation (FAST) Act. Los Angeles County is one example of a region that expanded its public transportation system using local, state, and federal funding.

## What Is the Public Health Issue?

Transportation systems help ensure that people can reach everyday destinations, such as jobs, schools, healthy food outlets and healthcare facilities, safely and reliably. Public transportation services play an important role for people who are unable to drive, including those without access to personal vehicles, children, individuals with disabilities, and older adults. The US transportation infrastructure focuses

## Fast Fact

**The leading cause of death among individuals 10 to 19 years old is accidental—62 percent from car accidents.**

on motor vehicle travel (e.g., passenger cars, vans, SUVs, pickup trucks, and other light trucks) and provides limited support for other transportation options. According to the US Census Bureau, in 2013 approximately 86 percent of all workers traveled to work by private vehicle, and 76 percent drove alone. Also in 2013, 69 percent of urban households and 14 percent of rural households had access to public transit. Although using public transportation has historically been safer than travel in passenger vehicles, passenger vehicle travel has grown more quickly than other modes of travel. Motor vehicle crashes continue to be the leading cause of injury-related death for many age groups. In 2013, motor vehicle crashes were the second leading cause of death among individuals aged 13 to 25 years.

Public transportation systems provide opportunities for increased physical activity in the form of walking or biking on either end of the trip (e.g., from home to bus stop or from train stop to office) and reduced motor vehicle travel. Despite these benefits, many Americans view walking and bicycling within their communities unfavorably because of barriers such as disability, age, chronic disease, inconvenience or safety concerns about traffic and a lack of sidewalks, crosswalks, and bicycle facilities. Many people aren't meeting the recommendations for physical activity; the lack of physical activity contributes to obesity, diabetes, heart disease, stroke, and other chronic health conditions in the US.

Air pollution from motor vehicles continues to contribute to adverse respiratory and cardiovascular health effects. Nitrogen oxides and volatile organic compounds react with sunlight to create ozone. Carbon monoxide, nitrogen oxides, and ozone are associated with a variety of health problems including myocardial ischemia, chest pain, coughing, throat irritation, and airway inflammation, and can worsen bronchitis, emphysema, and asthma. Particulate matter, which is produced by engine exhaust and tire and brake wear, is associated with an increased risk of respiratory and cardiovascular disease.

## What Is the Evidence of Health Impact and Cost Effectiveness?

Public transportation systems are associated with reductions in several health risk factors such as motor vehicle crashes, air pollution, and physical inactivity. The US Department of Transportation reported that public transportation (school, intercity, transit bus, light rail transit, and subway) accounted for less than one percent of transportation fatalities in 2011, while private passenger vehicles accounted for more than 75 percent of transportation fatalities. An analysis of the transportation fatality risk in the US found that the fatality rates per billion passenger miles traveled between 2000 and 2009 were 0.11 for buses, 0.24 for urban mass transit rail trains, 0.43 for passengers on commuter rails, and 7.28 for drivers or passengers in a car or light truck. For every passenger mile traveled, public transportation produces only a fraction of the harmful pollution of private vehicles: only five percent as much carbon monoxide, less than eight percent as many volatile organic compounds, and nearly half as much carbon dioxide and nitrogen oxides.

A systematic review examining public transportation use and physical activity found that use of public transport was associated with an additional 8 to 33 minutes of walking per day. A study of the impact of adding light rail stations in Los Angeles found it to be associated with an increase in daily physical activity among residents with previously lower physical activity levels. The expansion was also associated with a reduction in vehicle miles traveled and their related emissions. Another study found that train commuters took an average of 30 percent more steps per day than car commuters. A study of 130 US cities found that each rail passenger mile represents a reduction of three to six automobile passenger miles—through direct substitution and indirectly through the creation of compact, mixed-use transit-oriented developments that foster walking and cycling and reduced automobile ownership. A final study, looking at zoning for TODs, found that this type of zoning was associated with significantly higher rates of public transportation to work and active transportation to work.

A descriptive cost analysis examined the value of the health benefits, which included fewer traffic crashes, less air pollution and increased physical fitness, of increasing the proportion of the population that has access to public transit. The analysis estimated that if a city with a typical quality North American public transit service improved to high quality (i.e., fast, convenient and comfortable) urban rail or bus rapid transit service, the per capita annual health benefits would be $355. If improvements were made to achieve a high quality transit service with walkable, mixed-use development around stations, the per capita annual health benefits would be $541. It also estimated that for a city with a million residents, an increase in the proportion of households located in transit-oriented developments from 10 percent to 20 percent would produce nearly $71 million of total annual health benefits, and an increase from 10 percent to 40 percent would generate more than $216 million of total annual health benefits.

A cost-benefit analysis that examined the impact of expanding public transportation capacity by converting a lane for bus rapid transit found an association with positive net benefits to society, including travel time savings, travel cost savings, and emissions reduction.

## EVALUATING THE AUTHOR'S ARGUMENTS:

**In this viewpoint the US Department of Health & Human Services makes a compelling case for expansion of public transportation. Using specific details from the viewpoint article chart the pros and cons of this argument.**

Viewpoint 3

# The Future of Transportation Is Already Here

*"In ten years, transportation in the United States will look far different than it does now."*

## Steffen Fuchs and Rafat Shehadeh

In the following viewpoint Steffen Fuchs and Rafat Shehadeh argue that transportation in the United States will be radically different in the not-so-distant future. The authors maintain that departments of transportation (DOTs) must change with these alterations. This may not be easy, as DOTs are not typically focused on innovation and experimentation. Steffen Fuchs is an expert in business and focuses on infrastructure, digital, and innovation for his clients. Rafat Shehadeh is an associate business partner.

**AS YOU READ, CONSIDER THE FOLLOWING QUESTIONS:**

1. How might roads be different in the future, according to the authors?
2. What five key areas must DOTs change in order to be ready for the future as reported by the viewpoint?
3. Is the future positive for DOTs according to Fuchs and Rafat?

In ten years, transportation in the United States will look far different than it does now. Already, vehicle-sharing and electrification are widespread; and autonomous vehicles (AVs) and the Internet of Things are poised to make even bigger waves.

"The Department of Transportation of the Future," by Steffen Fuchs and Rafat Shehadeh, McKinsey & Company, October 2017. Reprinted by permission.

Physical infrastructure will evolve to reflect this. For instance, roads could be stacked with lanes dedicated to specific types of traffic, such as commuter cars, commercial vehicles, AVs, and bicycles. Drones will deliver goods to homes and businesses, and the number of charging stations constructed for electric vehicles will surge.

These changes are imminent—and they have sweeping implications for the entities that govern transportation infrastructure. If the face of transportation will change in just a decade, and large transport infrastructure projects can take more than a decade to complete, then departments of transportation (DOTs) have little more than three to five years to adapt. Those DOTs that focus on older travel models will be unprepared to serve new kinds of demand. They will also be slower to convert growing data sets into actionable plans and projects that further support these changing trends. Conversely, those that proactively embrace change have the opportunity to shape the future of transportation as well as urban, suburban, and rural development.

Adjusting to these rapid advances and providing effective, next-generation solutions requires agility and radical innovation. This kind of disruption can challenge the culture of DOTs—many of which are required to focus on compliance and reducing risk, not encouraging experimentation. Furthermore, DOTs rely heavily on their legislatures and stakeholders to deliver on their plans. A lack of support from these stakeholders affects their funding and operating model. These challenges make it difficult to adapt quickly or act decisively to execute broad transformation.

Yet transformation will be necessary for DOTs to deliver safe, reliable, and integrated infrastructure. No blanket solution exists, as each DOT is organized and governed differently. However, we see a shared vision and set of guiding principles that all DOTs can aspire to follow in paving their own path.

## The Current Plight of the Typical DOT

While some DOTs are already adapting to impending change, it's possible that some are still primarily focused on meeting their present budgetary needs and securing funding to solve traditional transportation problems such as maintaining highways or building bridges. These DOTs may not have the capacity to invest in new innovation.

*The overcrowded highways of today could give way to innovative transportation network systems unlike any we've seen before.*

Similarly, public stakeholders such as metropolitan planning organizations (MPOs) are just as central in the overall planning process as the states and often have different priorities.

One key reason for favoring conventional solutions is that the DOT workforce, although changing, is still heavily dominated by civil engineers. While this talent will always be critical to the success of large civil works organizations, there is always a risk of groupthink when an organization is mostly composed of people with similar training and problem-solving approaches. Additionally, many DOT functions operate in silos.

The life of a project—from planning to finance to engineering to right-of-way and permitting to construction—is excessively linear. Each group manages its own portfolio with too little cross-function integration. The combination of these factors can limit a DOT's ability to evolve beyond its existing model.

## A Road Map to the DOT of the Future

To acquire the necessary skills and transform its practices, a DOT must implement changes to five core capabilities: strategy, portfolio

**FAST FACT**

**A Pew Research survey found that 9 percent of people interviewed wouldn't want an autonomous vehicle because they like the act of driving.**

planning, its resources model, project planning and delivery, and performance measurement.

### 1. A Strategy That Supports Funding Priorities and Enables Agility and Innovation

DOTs must work closely with their partners—such as MPOs and local municipalities—to educate and inform the public about the impending changes to the world of transportation. This will serve two purposes: to garner broad support and to instill urgency in public officials to unlock funding for programs needed to propel DOTs through this evolutionary process. DOTs can also partner with other public and private organizations to gather and fund innovative ideas.

One leading DOT created a technology task force to uncover new tools and strategies that would enhance the state's transportation system while positioning the state as an economic and technological leader. The task force consults with industry experts and leading institutions to identify impactful emerging technologies, while conducting research to build a fact base that informs change.

### 2. Portfolio Planning That Includes Scenarios for All Potential Transportation Solutions, Not Just Conventional Roads and Bridges

The problem of congestion creates a particularly urgent need for new scenario planning—one that is felt most acutely in cities. This planning is not just about building more roads or wider lanes; it's about envisioning scenarios that incorporate specific new solutions such as AVs, bicycles, and ride sharing.

DOTs would benefit from an integrated portfolio that allows stakeholders to see, track, and understand all the work being funded, enabling real-time decision making. This portfolio could improve scenario planning, allowing funds to be used more efficiently to find the best solutions to current and future problems. DOTs could also work more closely with their cities and MPO partners to develop a clearer understanding of the city's overall socioeconomic priorities—bolstering the logistics industry, for example, or preventing suburban flight—and how transportation can inform and achieve those goals.

## 3. A Resources Model That Creates the Human Engine to Fuel Innovation

DOTs will have to evolve from a predominantly engineering-focused culture to one that integrates classical engineering, new engineering skills, technology capabilities, general problem solving, and financial acumen. To succeed, they'll need a talent acquisition and development plan that speaks to a generation of innovators interested in making a positive impact on their communities. Of course, these innovators will still need traditional engineering teams. But DOTs of the future will rely heavily on data scientists that analyze disparate information streams and develop solutions that incorporate AVs and other emerging mobility trends.

They may also create teams of programmers that develop apps to communicate live traffic information to drivers' cars and mobile devices. The key will be for DOTs to provide the right organizational structure that successfully blends new skills with the old to drive fruitful outcomes.

## 4. Project Planning and Delivery That Produces Effective Solutions Quickly

For today's DOTs, delivering on time and within budget is at times simply an exercise in managing contractors and getting plans out the door. Technology will change this process with digital solutions that develop more accurate cost and schedule estimates, incorporate data analytics from hundreds of other similar projects, and codify on-the-ground experience into true organizational knowledge. Digital tools can also monitor equipment and crew efficiency, which in turn will transform contractor management and boost productivity. Embracing these technologies may seem daunting for some of today's DOTs, but those that do so will reap significant value.

While full digital transformation is not yet a reality for many DOTs, some are moving in the right direction. One DOT launched a portfolio and project management initiative that consolidates multiple management systems into one standardized platform. Moving from disparate systems to a single repository of information creates efficiency, accuracy, and transparency that improves the agency's decision-making and forecasting abilities. Such a system can also lay the foundation for future integrated solutions and apps, equipping DOTs to embrace long-term digitization.

## 5. Performance Measurement That Supports the Vision

Performance management today is often too focused on tracking engineering errors, cost overruns, and delays. To support long-term evolution and growth, the sector will need to move away from these metrics and consider the broader goal of a better transportation system. For example, DOTs should be evaluated against the efficacy of their solutions, not the money they disburse, and chief engineers should be rewarded based on their improvements to road networks and other transport solutions. A number of DOTs are already at the forefront of this evolution, but much more needs to be done.

## Looking Forward

Today, a United States without interstate highways seems unimaginable—but it was not long ago that DOTs were preparing for and acclimating to nationwide transformation. Radical innovation will be challenging; yet it has been done before, and it can be done again. DOT leaders should acknowledge that the imminent changes to transportation are about to redefine their existing structure and models. They should be visionary, pragmatic, bold, and courageous in the years ahead, and stakeholders must coalesce to support them in their transformation. With these measures firmly in place, DOTs can act today to establish a sturdy foundation for the future.

## EVALUATING THE AUTHOR'S ARGUMENTS:

**In this viewpoint Steffen Fuchs and Rafat Shehadeh maintain that changes are coming to the future of transportation. Which of three future transportation visions—autonomous vehicles, bicycling, or ride sharing—do you see yourself using the most? Why?**

Viewpoint 4

# Roads Must Be Improved to Accommodate Self-Driving Cars

*"The key question is not when will self-driving cars be ready for the roads, but rather which roads will be ready for self-driving cars."*

**Nick Oliver, Kristina Potočnik, and Thomas Calvard**

In the following viewpoint Nick Oliver, Kristina Potočnik, and Thomas Calvard present an overview of the state of self-driving cars and the environment that this technology must master. The authors contend that there is still much work and testing that must equip the cars to become safe and trustworthy. They outline what the transition might look like from mostly human driven cars to autonomous cars. Nick Oliver, Kristina Potočnik, and Thomas Calvard all are affiliated with the University of Edinburgh Business School.

**AS YOU READ, CONSIDER THE FOLLOWING QUESTIONS:**

1. What are positive and negative conditions associated with self-driving cars?
2. What other transportation sector do the authors compare to self-driving cars?
3. Which controlled environments will support self-driving cars?

"To Make Self-Driving Cars Safe, We Also Need Better Roads and Infrastructure," by Nick Oliver, Kristina Potočnik and Thomas Calvard, Harvard Business School, August 14, 2018. Reprinted by permission.

The big question around self-driving cars, for many people, is: When will the technology be ready? In other words, when will autonomous vehicles be safe enough to operate on their own? But there has been far less attention paid to two equally important questions: When will the driving environment be ready to accommodate self-driving cars? And where will this technology work best?

Self-driving cars are the most challenging automation project ever undertaken. Driving requires a great deal of processing and decision making, which must be automated. On top of that, there are many unpredictable external factors that must be accounted for, and therefore many ways in which the driving environment must change.

Cars are heavy, fast-moving objects, operating in public spaces. Safety is largely the responsibility of the driver, who must continuously observe, analyze, decide, and act. Not only do drivers have to follow the rules of the road, but they also have to communicate with each other and other road users to navigate ambiguous or contested situations; think about how you wave or nod to someone to signal "You go first."

Self-driving systems have to execute all of these functions, and do so accurately, reliably, and safely, across a wide variety of situations and conditions. Currently, the technology is more capable in some situations than in others.

Through sensors and detailed mapping software, the systems build representations of their environments and update them many times a second. They classify the objects they see and predict their likely behavior before selecting appropriate responses. The speed and the accuracy of these systems already surpass human responses in many situations. Lasers can see in the dark. Reaction times can be nearly instantaneous.

But some conditions still constrain them. Cameras are challenged by strong, low-angle sunlight (important for reading traffic lights), and lasers can be confused by fog and snowfall. Unusual, unfamiliar, and unstructured situations (so-called edge cases), such as accidents, road work, or a fast-approaching emergency response vehicle, can be hard to classify. And self-driving systems are not good at detecting

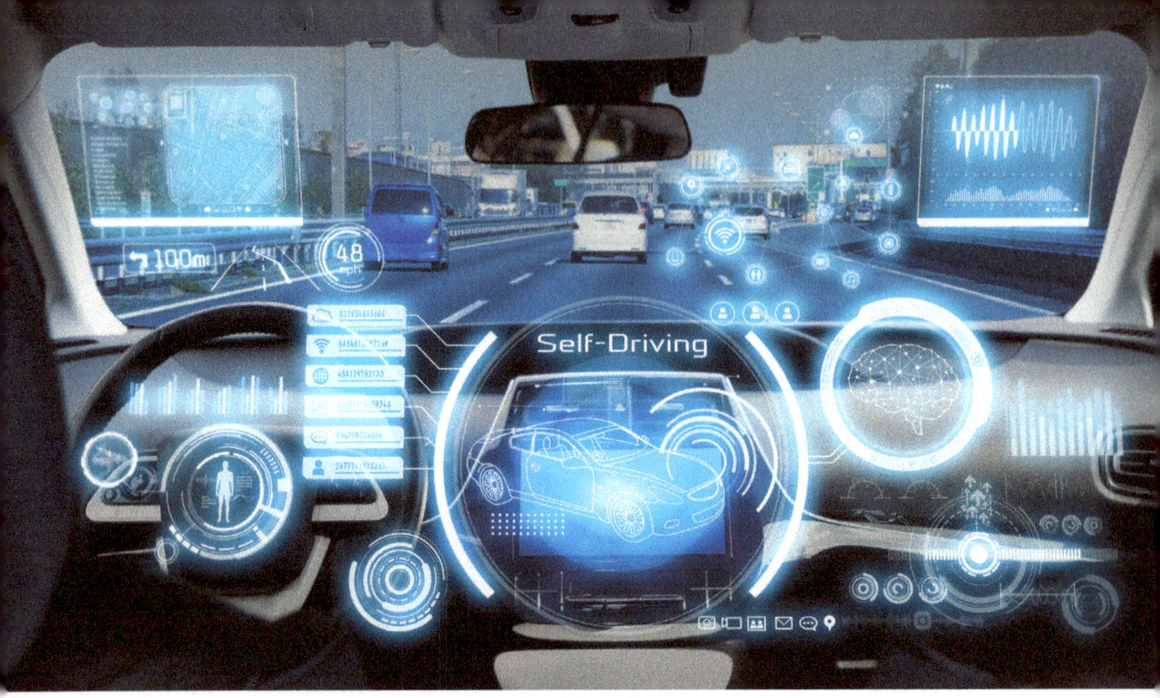


*In the future, your car's dashboard could look like this.*

and interpreting human cues, such as gestures and eye contact, that facilitate coordination between cars on the road.

Processes and environments that are structured well are much easier to automate than those that are not. Automated systems need to collect, classify, and respond to information, and this is easier to do in a clean, unambiguous environment—which is what many driving environments are not. The designers of self-driving systems simply cannot foresee every possible combination of conditions that will occur on the road. (Though companies are trying: Google's Waymo team deliberately subjects its cars to "pathological situations" that are unlikely to happen, such as people hiding in bags and then jumping in front of the car.)

Over time, learning will take place and the number of situations that systems cannot recognize will decrease. In fact, learning is likely to be better in an automated system, because once an incident has occurred and is understood, the fix can be rolled out across all vehicles. Currently, learning is largely confined to individual drivers, and is not shared across the system as a whole. But novel combinations of conditions will never be eliminated, and sometimes these will have catastrophic consequences—a pattern seen even in the highly disciplined environment of commercial aviation.

The problem therefore lies in our period of transition. For the technology to improve, it must be exposed to real, on-road conditions. In the early stages of deployment, it sometimes won't know the best way to respond and therefore will have to hand over control to a human driver. The issue here, however, is that humans zone out when their full attention is not needed. As self-driving cars improve and humans intervene less, driver inattention and the associated problem of quickly reengaging to respond become even bigger problems.

And as the technology becomes more sophisticated, the situations where it requires human assistance are likely to be more complex, ambiguous, and difficult to diagnose. In these cases, a startled human has much less chance of responding correctly. Even in the highly sterile environment of an aircraft cockpit, pilots can be caught by surprise and respond incorrectly when automation has ceded control.

Two fatal accidents involving Tesla vehicles operating on their Autopilot systems demonstrate how this space between semi-automated driving and intermittent human control may be the most dangerous place of all. In the Florida 2016 crash, the driver of the Tesla had his hands on the steering wheel for only 25 seconds of the 37 minutes in which he operated the vehicle in automated control mode. In California in 2018, the driver's hands were not detected on the steering wheel in the six seconds preceding the crash.

This problem has led companies such as Waymo and Ford to advocate for fully autonomous cars that get rid of the need for handovers. But this requires a leap: With no driver as backup, there is a risk that the technology will be catapulted into environments that are beyond its ability to handle.

Self-driving cars also have to navigate an environment that is shared—with pedestrians who sometimes cross the road without looking, cyclists, animals, debris, inanimate objects, and of course whatever elements the weather brings. Road infrastructure, regulations, and driving customs vary from country to country, even city to city, and are overseen by a multiplicity of bodies. So it's not clear which institutions have the power and reach to regulate and standardize the driving environment, if they even exist. Roads are very different from airspace, which is governed by powerful global regulatory bodies, has far less traffic, and has very high licensing standards for pilots.

This means that we need to think not just about the onboard technology but also about the environment in which it is deployed. We'll likely start to see a more standardized and active environment as more smart infrastructure is constructed. Think of radio transmitters replacing traffic lights, higher-capacity mobile and wireless data networks handling both vehicle-to-vehicle and vehicle-to-infrastructure communication, and roadside units providing real-time data on weather, traffic, and other conditions. Common protocols and communications standards will have to be devised and negotiated, as they were with internet communication protocols or the Global System for Mobile Communications (GSM) for mobile phones. This transition will take decades, and autonomous vehicles will have to share the roads with human drivers.

If rapid, radical change to the driving environment is impractical, what is the alternative? The most likely near-term scenario we'll see are various forms of spatial segregation: Self-driving cars will operate in some areas and not others. We're already seeing this, as early trials of the technology are taking place in designated test areas or in relatively simple, fair-weather environments. But we may also see dedicated lanes or zones for self-driving vehicles, both to give them a more structured environment while the technology is refined and to protect other road users from their limitations.

We can also expect to see self-driving cars deployed first in relatively controlled environments (such as theme parks, private campuses, and retirement villages), where speeds are lower and the range of situations the vehicles have to deal with is limited. Economics, too, will play an important role in where and how self-driving cars begin to operate. The vehicles will likely appear in environments where it is cost-effective to develop and maintain highly detailed mapping, such as dense urban environments, although of course these also pose other challenges due to their complexity.

Although the cost of self-driving cars will fall once they enter mass production, it is currently very high, from \$250,000 to \$300,000 a vehicle, according to some estimates. So they will first appear in settings where vehicle utilization rates are high and where the cost of a driver's time matters—imagine robotaxis or ride-hailing vehicles operating in defined, geo-fenced zones. Trials of these are already under way. Robotaxis also point to a way in which humans can support self-driving technology while avoiding the human zone-out problem by interacting with call centers. A self-driving vehicle that cannot get past an obstruction in the road without acting illegally (crossing a white line, for example) can stop and call a human operator for advice, who can then authorize it to act in a nonstandard way.

## Fast Fact

**Only 11 percent of adults in the United States feel very safe sharing the road with self-driving cars, according to Pew Research.**

In the long run, driverless cars will help us reduce accidents, save time spent on commuting, and make more people mobile. The onboard technology is developing rapidly, but we're entering a transition stage in which we need to think carefully about how it will interact with human drivers and the wider driving environment. During this period, the key question we should be asking is not when will self-driving cars be ready for the roads, but rather which roads will be ready for self-driving cars.

## EVALUATING THE AUTHOR'S ARGUMENTS:

**In this viewpoint, authors Nick Oliver, Kristina Potočnik, and Thomas Calvard present an overview of the state of self-driving cars. Should the development of self-driving cars be slowed since most adults in the United States are not comfortable with this technology? Why or why not?**

Viewpoint 5

# The Internet of Things Poses a Threat to Security

*"If someone wanted to hack into these global information networks, IoT devices provide billions of extra entry points."*

## Tim Stevens

In the following viewpoint Tim Stevens analyzes the issue of national security and how it is being affected by an ever-increasing level of technology. Stevens argues that many devices that belong to the Internet of Things (IoT) are inherently dangerous because they are easy to hack and in turn provide a way for hackers or others intent on causing harm a way to access large systems that could cause great harm to countries and their citizens. Stevens wonders whether governments should get involved and require regulations aimed at preventing potential problems. Tim Stevens lectures about global security issues at King's College in London.

### AS YOU READ, CONSIDER THE FOLLOWING QUESTIONS:

1. What are IoT devices, according to the viewpoint?
2. What is a botnet?
3. What is a fear of cyber-security professionals, according to the viewpoint?

"Internet of Things: When Objects Threaten National Security," by Tim Stevens, The Conversation, May 28, 2019. https://theconversation.com/internet-of-things-when-objects-threaten-national-security-96962. Licensed under CC BY-ND 4.0 International.

We all know personal devices can be hacked, but a whole country's security could be at risk too. With the rise of the so-called Internet of Things (IoT), and against the backdrop of cyberwarfare, digital surveillance and digital subversion, the risk to national security is increasing. Earlier this year the head of the UK National Cyber Security Centre publicly stated that a major cyber-attack on the country's essential services was a question of "when, not if".

The IoT comprises of the billions of online objects embedded in our homes, workplaces and cities, that are constantly collecting, analysing and transmitting data. Some IoT devices, such as personal fitness trackers or smartphones, are carried with us wherever we go. Others we interact with remotely, such as domestic heating controls. Many are invisible, operating silently to modulate traffic flows, industrial control systems, and much more.

IoT devices are not so much things with computers in them, but computers with things attached to them. Because no computer is perfectly secure, that means that neither is your smart fridge or your virtual assistant. Like all things online, these objects form part of massively distributed networks. If someone wanted to hack into these global information networks, IoT devices provide billions of extra entry points.

It is relatively easy to hack an IoT device, as many cheap products do not have adequate security. Even devices with advanced security, such as driverless cars, are vulnerable. This means that IoT technologies are widely regarded as a major cyber-security problem. Pacemakers being hacked, air traffic control systems going down, and all out "cyber-war" are just some worst case scenarios. Vulnerabilities, if exploited, could lead to damage, injury and death.

Cyber-attacks on critical national infrastructure are already a very real threat. In 2015, the Ukranian power grid was affected by a cyber-attack that left Kiev without electricity for several hours. More recently in 2017, the UK's NHS was compromised for weeks due to the malicious software (malware) WannaCry.

These incidents show just how disruptive cyber-attacks can be and the fact that IoT attacks are proliferating and diversifying is a cause to worry. One major internet security company reported that

*Air traffic control may be vulnerable to cyberattacks. Government agencies must be on guard constantly to ensure systems are updated and secure.*

IoT attacks increased 600% in 2016–17. This is an exponential rise and is expected to persist, not least as the number of IoT devices increase. Devices already outnumbered humans in 2017 but may top 20 billion by 2020.

## The Rise of the Botnet

A botnet is a network of internet connected devices that have been hacked, hijacked and controlled remotely. The problem is that poorly secured IoT accounts make perfect targets for hackers attempting to develop and weaponise botnets. With the right malware, hackers can use botnets to perform distributed denial-of-service (DDoS) attacks against specific targets. The malware uses thousands of devices to flood internet servers with traffic and disable access to online resources. Billions of IoT devices make it easier for hackers to take control of large botnets and attack even the most robust targets.

The Mirai malware exploited vulnerabilities in IoT devices, such as CCTV cameras and routers, to do just this. In October 2016, Mirai launched a DDoS against Dyn, Inc, the company that provides access to major platforms like Twitter, Amazon and Netflix.

The DDoS prevented consumers from accessing these platforms for several hours. Of course, it is difficult to calculate the financial implications of such incidents but Mirai showed how essential services can be attacked by exploiting IoT devices.

> **FAST FACT**
>
> In response to a 2014 canvassing of experts by Pew Research, 83 percent said that by 2025, the IoT will have a widespread and beneficial effect on the everyday lives of people.

States or non-state actors could try and use an IoT botnet to attack a country's health, energy, transport or finance sector. If a botnet were directed against critical national infrastructure, the effects could be severe. Speculation in the absence of evidence is rarely wise but it is not hard to imagine what might happen if financial services were taken offline, or rail transport networks sabotaged. No cyber-attack has yet collapsed the global financial system, or killed anyone, thankfully, but these are the fears of policymakers and cyber-security professionals.

Attribution is not easy either but it's getting better. Were a state or terrorist group identified as the perpetrator of a major attack, national security apparatuses should swing into action to counter them. For NATO members, a cyber-attack might even trigger a collective political and military response.

## How Are Governments Responding?

So far both the US and the UK have stopped short of introducing regulation, but instead are putting pressure on businesses to make their products more secure. However, these policies do not address the overarching problem: companies will keep on selling products with poor security because consumers are willing to buy them. It is supply and demand. There are presently few incentives for firms to bring IoT products to market that meet high security standards. In global supply chains, the picture is even more complicated because national initiatives cannot resolve transnational problems.

The market will not solve this problem, so more robust government regulation is all but inevitable. Few bureaucracies relish the challenge. In policy terms, this is a "wicked problem." Even if a solution was obvious, it would likely be impossible due to key players' competing motives and the dynamism of the technical environment.

A more radical approach is to address why the IoT exists in the first place. It is the product of both laudable aims (energy efficiency, public welfare) and an obsession with connectivity for connectivity's sake. As is well-established, complex systems generate unpredictable effects. If we are to minimise the risks of wiring up our world, we need to consider prioritising devices that are truly necessary over ones that are simply desirable. This will require a fundamental shift in mindset, putting the public good before profit and political expediency.

## EVALUATING THE AUTHOR'S ARGUMENTS:

**In this viewpoint Tim Stevens informs the reader of the state of the IoT and how this technology is a potential security nightmare. What devices are in your home that are connected via the IoT's? Have you experienced any problems associated with this technology? Does this cause you to think twice about purchasing technology enabled items?**

# Facts About Transportation Infrastructure

Editor's note: These facts can be used in reports to add credibility when making important points or claims.

## Condition of Transportation Infrastructure

Report Card issued by the ASCE, American Society of Civil Engineers

- The first report was issued in 1998. Reports are issued every four years.
- 28 civil engineers determine the "grade" given to American infrastructure.
- Reports on 16 different infrastructures including aviation, bridges, dams, drinking water, energy, hazardous waste, inland waterways, levees, ports, public parks & recreation, rail, roads, schools, solid waste, transit, and wastewater.
- Average grade given in 1998 was a "D", in 2017, a "D+."

## US Department of Transportation

- January 12, 1966, President Lyndon B. Johnson announces intention to create DOT.
- Established by an act of Congress on October 15, 1966.
- January 16, 1967, Alan S. Boyd sworn in as first Secretary DOT.
- February 1, 1983, Elizabeth H. Dole becomes first woman to serve as Secretary DOT.
- Covers automobiles, aviation, railroads, trucks & motorcoaches, bicycles, public transport, boating, and roadways & bridges.

## Highway Transportation Facts

- President Dwight D. Eisenhower signed the Federal-Aid Highway Act on June 29, 1956, which made way for the Interstate Highway System.

- Vehicle miles driven increased in 2018 while fatality rate decreased (lowest since 2014).
- December 4, 2015, President Obama signs the FAST Act (Fixing America's Surface Transportation) which gave $305 billion to fix transportation systems.
- In 2018, 36,560 people were killed in traffic crashes.

## Air Transport Facts

- December 1958, the Federal Aviation Agency begins operations.
- December 2003, Century of Aviation Reauthorization Act, proposed to put into place an air transportation system for the future, the Next Generation Air Transportation System.
- US skies are filled with around 7,000 flights at any one time.
- Aviation is the safest form of travel.

## Rail Travel Facts

- On July 1, 1862 Abraham Lincoln signed the Pacific Railway Act aimed at building a US railroad connecting the Atlantic to the Pacific. Thousands of immigrants built this Transcontinental Railroad, which was completed on May 10, 1869 with a final "Golden Spike" driven into place.
- From 2012 to 2015 commuter ridership increased.

## Public Transportation Facts

- Public transportation encompasses buses, subways, streetcars & trolleys, commuter trains, cable cars, van service, ferries & water taxis, and transit services.
- Americans took 9.9 billion trips on public transportation in 2018.
- Traveling by public transport is 10 times safer than traveling by automobile.
- Traveling by public transportation saves gasoline by about 4.2 billion gallons of gas per year in the United States.
- On average US households spend 16 cents out of every dollar on their cars.
- By living with one less car, a household could save $10,000.

# Organizations to Contact

The editors have compiled the following list of organizations concerned with the issues debated in this book. The descriptions are derived from materials provided by the organizations. All have publications or information available for interested readers. The list was compiled on the date of publication of the present volume; the information provided here may change. Be aware that many organizations take several weeks or longer to respond to inquiries, so allow as much time as possible for the receipt of requested materials.

**American Road & Transportation Builders Association (ARTBA)**
250 E. Street SW, Suite 900, Washington DC, 20024
(202) 289-4434
website: www.artba.org/
The ARTBA is a federation which has one main goal: to aggressively grow and protect transportation infrastructure in the United States, to meet the demand for safe and efficient travel.

**Federal Aviation Administration (FAA)**
800 Independence Avenue SW, Washington DC, 20591
(866) 835-5322
website: www.faa.gov/
The FAA is an agency of the US government which has a mission to provide the United States with the safest aerospace system in the world.

**Federal Highway Administration (FHWA)**
1200 New Jersey Avenue SE, Washington DC, 20590
(202) 366-4000
website: www.fhwa.dot.gov/
The FHWA is a governmental agency that supports state and local governments in maintaining and improving the highway system of the United States.

### Federal Railroad Administration (FRA)

1200 New Jersey Avenue SE, Washington, DC 20590
(202) 366-4000
website: www.railroads.dot.gov/
The FRA oversees and provides the safe, reliable, and efficient movement of goods and people over the US system of railroads.

### National Highway Traffic Safety Administration (NHTSA)

1200 New Jersey Avenue SE, Washington DC, 20590
(888) 327-4236
email: Use link on contact page
website: www.nhtsa.gov/
The NHTSA is a governmental agency that is responsible for keeping people safe on America's roadways.

### National Transportation Safety Board (NTSB)

490 L'Enfant Plaza SW, Washington, DC 20594
(202) 314-6000
website: www.ntsb.gov/
The NTSB is a governmental agency that investigates accidents occurring in the United States concerning aviation, marine, railroad, highway, pipeline, and hazardous materials.

### Transportation for America (t4america)

1152 15th Street NW, Suite 450, Washington, DC, 20005
(202) 955-5543
email: info@t4america.org
website: t4america.org/
This organization is made up of state, local, and regional leaders aiming to advocate for a safe and affordable US transportation system.

### US Department of Transportation (DOT)

1200 New Jersey Avenue SE, Washington DC, 20590
(202) 366-4000
website: www.transportation.gov/about
DOT is responsible for making the US transportation system the most efficient, modern, and safe in the world.

# For Further Reading

## Books

Blue, Elly. *Bikenomics*. Portland, OR: Microcosm Publishing, 2013. Critiques America's culture of the car. Encourages and explores the realities of why biking is better.

Friss, Evan. *On Bicycles: A 200 Year Old History of Cycling in New York City*. New York: Columbia University Press, 2019. Explore why cycling is so important to the city of New York in the past and to the present day.

Gallamore, Robert E. *American Railroads: Decline and Renaissance in the Twentieth Century.* Cambridge, MA: Harvard University Press, 2016. Railroads were once a popular mode of travel, but by the beginning of the twentieth century they lost out to other modes of transportation.

Kanter, Rosabeth Moss. *Move: How to Rebuild and Reinvent America's Infrastructure*. New York: W. W. Norton & Company, 2016. Americans are stuck with undesirable transportation infrastructure. Read about the people and projects across America that are changing transportation for the better.

Newquist, H. P. *From Here to There: The Story of How We Transport Ourselves and Everything Else*. New York: Smithsonian, 2017. Learn about the history of transportation, from primitive beginnings up to driverless vehicles.

Petroski, Henry. *The Road Taken: The History and Future of America's Infrastructure*. New York: Bloomsbury, 2016. Read about the history of America's highway system, to the American Society of Civil Engineers and their report card on failing infrastructure, to the pot holes plaguing everyone's streets.

Schwartz, Samuel I. *No One at the Wheel: Driverless Cars and the Road of the Future*. New York: Public Affairs, 2018. Written by an expert on US transportation issues, this book analyzes how driverless cars will change the entire infrastructure and driving scene.

## Periodicals and Internet Sources


Barber, Megan, "9 US Transportation Projects to Watch in 2018," Curbed, January 18, 2018. https://www.curbed.com/2018/1/18/16898246/transportation-construction-projects-biggest-us-2018.

Baroud, Hiba, "Measuring Up US Infrastructure Against Other Countries," The Conversation, February 13, 2018. https://theconversation.com/measuring-up-us-infrastructure-against-other-countries-78164.

Chandran, Kavita, "The 'Internet of Things' Will Cause More Security Problems Next Year, Exec Warns," CNBC, November 29, 2018. https://www.cnbc.com/2018/11/29/internet-of-things-will-cause-security-problems-next-year-says-exec.html.

DePillis, Lydia, "Trump Unveils Infrastructure Plan," CNN BUSINESS, February 12, 2018. https://money.cnn.com/2018/02/11/news/economy/trump-infrastructure-plan-details/index.html.

Eisenstein, Paul, "Not Everyone is Ready to Ride as Autonomous Vehicles Take to the Road in Every-Increasing Numbers," CNBC, October 14, 2018. https://www.cnbc.com/2018/10/14/self-driving-cars-take-to-the-road-but-not-everyone-is-ready-to-ride.html.

Howard, Jacqueline, "A Wake-Up Call About What's Killing America's Young People," CNN, June 1, 2018. https://www.cnn.com/2018/06/01/health/youth-injury-death-rate-cdc-study/index.html.

Lardieri, Alexa, "Report: Two-Thirds of World's Population Will Live in Cities by 2050," *U.S. News*, May 17, 2018. https://www.usnews.com/news/world/articles/2018-0517/report-two-thirds-of-worlds-population-will-live-in-cities-by-2050.

Malinsky, Gilli, "The 10 Most Expensive Infrastructure Projects in the US," Bankrate, February 9, 2017. https://www.bankrate.com/banking/savings/the-10-most-expensive-infrastructure-projects-in-the-us/#slide=1.

Marshall, Aarian, "The 7 Most Majestic Infrastructure Projects of 2016," *Wired*, January 3, 2017. https://www.wired.com/2017/01/7-majestic-infrastructure-projects-2016/.

McArdle, Megan, "Why the United States Will Never Have High Speed Rail," *Washington Post*, February 12, 2019. https://www.washingtonpost.com/opinions/2019/02/13/why-united-states-will-never-have-high-speed-rail/.

Schaper, David, "10 Years After Bridge Collapse, America is Still Crumbling," NPR, August 1, 2017. https://www.npr.org/2017/08/01/540669701/10-years-after-bridge-collapse-america-is-still-crumbling.

Schaper, David, "Trump to Unveil Long-Awaited $1.5 Trillion Infrastructure Plan," NPR, February 11, 2018. https://www.npr.org/2018/02/11/584940681/trump-to-unveil-long-awaited-1-5-trillion-infrastructure-plan.

Woodyard, Chris, "Fewer Americans Bike to Work Despite New Trails, Lanes, and Bicycle Share Programs," *USA Today*, January 2, 2019. https://www.usatoday.com/story/news/nation/2019/01/02/bike-work-fewer-americans-new-trails-share-programs/2319972002/.

## Websites

**National Park System—Route 66**
**(www.nps.gov/nr/travel/route66/index.html)**
US Highway 66 is also known as "Route 66" or the "Mother Road." This highway is known for its historic sites and interesting things to see and do along 2,400 miles (3,862 kilometers), which stretch across almost two-thirds of the US continent.

**National Scenic Byways (www.fhwa.dot.gov/byways/)**
The site of the National Scenic Byways and All-American Roads has an interactive map that highlights highways across the United States. Noted highways have archaeological, historic, natural, cultural, recreational, and scenic specialties.

**2017 Infrastructure Report Card**
**(www.infrastructurereportcard.org/)**
Every four years the American Society of Civil Engineers, ASCE, issues a report card on the condition of American infrastructure. This site thoroughly analyzes and explains the current and historical reports issued.

# Index

# Picture Credits

Cover Suwin/Shutterstock.com; p. 10 Ann Cecil/Lonely Planet Images/Getty Images; p. 13 © iStockphoto.com/Andrei Stanescu; p. 27 NurPhoto/Getty Images; p. 34 Ulrich Baumgarten/Getty Images; p. 39 AhXiong/Shutterstock.com; p. 43 © iStockphoto .com/gladassfanny; p. 46 Malgosia S/Shutterstock.com; p. 50 Charles Wetegrove/EyeEm/Getty Images; p. 57 Travel Ink/Gallo Images/ Getty Images; p. 63 JayLazarin/iStock Unreleased/Getty Images; p. 69 Bloomberg/Getty Images; p. 76 ChandraDhas/iStock Unreleased/ Getty Images; p. 78 zhu difeng/Shutterstock.com; pp. 81, 98 metamorworks/Shutterstock.com; p. 85 SolStock/E+/Getty Images; p. 91 Pete Seaward/Stone/Getty Images; p. 104 Steve Parsons/PA Images/ Getty Images.